Jourı

W.

CHAPTER ONE

Donald lay along the banks of the river laughing as he tried to guddle a trout; he had his hand underwater trying to catch the fish which he knew was hiding under the overhanging bank. His pal Hamish was kneeling behind him pretending to push him in. Donald's sister Mary was standing back watching the two friends, they often played by the river when they were not at school, today they were on holiday, the sun was shining and they were having great fun splashing by the riverside. Hamish and Donald were great friends, they did everything together, Mary had attached herself to the boys when they had left that morning, she liked to play with the boys; they were always more adventurous and she was a bit of a tomboy. They were all roughly dressed in dull grey; Mary in a long dress trimmed with coloured ribbon, the boys in jerkins and trousers with a plain linen shift and heavy boots.

The two boys were quite different; Hamish was about a year older than Donald and the taller of the two, he had shorn fair hair and blue eyes. Donald was slightly built with black hair, and a much slimmer physique; he was a bit of a thinker, he would take the more intellectual approach rather than physical, he thought, Hamish acted. Hamish lived with his mother and father Agnes and Archie McLeod he also had a younger sister and two brothers.

The children lived in Strathgowan. A purpose built community about thirty miles south of Inverness, there was a lot of building going on and the town was made up of a main street and a square at one end, it was separated from the river by a small wood. Donald and Mary had another sister Hilda and a brother called Colin and they lived with their mother Jean Grant in a small house in one of the many back streets. Their mother was a small woman, at one time slim but she had gained weight and was getting slightly buxom, like her children she too dressed in the same drab colourless clothing despite the fact that she made her living as a seamstress to a local shopkeeper. Her wage was poor but she usually managed to make do, most of her wage went on food, but the children would often collected surplus vegetables from nearby farmers or stale bread from the local shops. She would sometimes get off cuts of coloured material from her employer which she used to brighten both her and the girls dresses by adding a fancy trim and making them a little less drab.

One of the boy's favourite pastimes was catching rabbits or they would try to get trout if they saw one hiding under the overhanging banks, they even tried to net a salmon, this was great fun for the boys and the extra food was always welcome. As the morning passed the children started to feel hungry so they set off home for dinner, but before leaving, Hamish and Donald set some snares between the woods and the side of the river. The two boys walked through the woods; the afternoon had turned hot, as they walked along a fine dust rose from the soft moss kicked up by their boots, Mary, who was annoyed that she had been left behind, had decided that she would follow, and was about one hundred yards behind them. As they came to the edge of the woods they checked the snare they had set there and were surprised to find that they had caught a rabbit, both boys were delighted and they were even more pleased when they found that they had caught three rabbits in their snares; supper tonight was going to be good. They approached the side of the river where they had set their last snare. Donald was carrying two rabbits and Hamish had the third, they could see that they had caught something; it was a pheasant, they had set the snare on a narrow rabbit run near the side of the river when they left the river bank that morning and now they saw the bird lying limp in the wire hoop. "Look Donald we've got a bird." shouted Hamish. As he ran forward he dropped the rabbit he was carrying to free the pheasant from the trap, it gave a reflex shudder, and then went limp; he disentangled it from the wire and shouted. "Donald look at this, we'll get some money for it down at the inn, imagine getting a pheasant." Donald looked at the bird, he was not sure about this, as it didn't feel right, "Yea but the old lady up at the big house better not find out about it or we'll be in trouble." "Och you're a fearty, this will give us some money, just think three rabbits and a pheasant," replied Hamish.

Across the river was the estate of the Countess of Badenoch where she bred pheasants for the autumn shoot and employed gamekeepers so that when the gentry came up to the estate in August there was plenty of birds. As far as the Countess was concerned taking a pheasant from the estate was poaching, this pheasant would be contraband. Mary had almost caught up with the boys when she saw that Hamish was holding up a bird, and she could also see the expression on Donald's face and decided that things were not quite right and held back. "We'll be in trouble if someone finds out that we caught a pheasant," said Donald. "I'm not going to tell them, and neither are you so how will they find out," replied Hamish. "Oh I know, but I'm not happy about it. I don't want to try and sell it." "Och I'll do that if you're feart." "It's alright for you, since my father died, my mother depends on me to help her. James is too young and so are Mary and Hilda, she says that we can catch but I think this pheasant could get us into trouble." "What happened to your father?" "He was working in the distillery up the road, but there was an accident and he was killed when a bag of grain fell on him. I was just wee at the time, but after that things were different, we don't have much money, so I have to do what I can to help." "I'm sorry Donald. Alright I'll go into the hotel, come on lets get going." Hamish picked up the pheasant and the rabbit and they set off for home, both thinking about their trophy but each in a different way, Mary, meanwhile had turned for home when they found the pheasant and was some distance ahead of them.

After a time Donald broke the silence, "Have you ever thought what you would like to do when you grow up?" "My Uncle Willie makes a lot of money," said Hamish. "I'd like to be like him, a mason, he's working on that new building up at the square, he always has plenty of money, and he's rich. What about you?" "I don't know. I think I would like to try and go to America," said Donald. He had ambitions but didn't tell Hamish. "But I don't know what I would like to do". The possibility of getting to America was like trying to get to the moon. In fact Donald had no idea where America was or how he would get there but it was a dream to hold on to. "How are you going to do that?" asked Hamish. "I don't know, but everyone who goes there gets rich," replied Donald. "How do you know that?" asked Hamish. "I've heard people talking about it." "What people?" "You know? People" He was optimistic and in his mind he would one day go to America and fulfil his dreams. Donald loved to draw but that would have been thought of as sissy to a would-be mason; Hamish already considered himself as a bit of a hard man. He would often be found with a pencil or charcoal in his hand and he drew as much as he could, he was not really interested in becoming rich, but at the back of his mind he thought that if he could fulfil his dream wealth would automatically follow.

As they continued their walk they heard a voice behind them, "Whit dea ye think yer doin wi that bird there ye young thieves?" Hamish, who was carrying the rabbit and the pheasant, tried to hide them behind his back. "Don't try to hide it; do you think I'm stupid?" "We were only catching rabbits," said Hamish. "So where did the bird come from?" "It got caught in a rabbit snare, we didn't try to catch it, it must have been caught in our snare," blurted Hamish. "Ye can tell that to the Countess, she will be the one to decide. But you lads are in trouble for stealing her property." Dewar, who was one of the Countess's gamekeepers, grabbed each of them roughly by the arm, and dragged them over the bridge to the north side of the river. He was a strong man and his grip on them was quite painful, they had no choice but to be dragged along with him.

CHAPTER 2

Jean Grant was proud of Donald and looked on him as the man of the house. Although only eleven he helped to provide some of the food, like the odd rabbit, and extra money when local farmers required extra hands, or when a shopkeeper required odd jobs around the shop. She was in her kitchen when Mary ran in, "Mother! Donald's up at the big house. They say that he stole a pheasant." Jean was shocked. Why would Donald be there, he was not a thief? "How do you know? Who told you?" "I was following them to the river and I saw Dewar the gamekeeper taking Donald and Hamish over to the Countesses estate Inchmohr he said that they had stolen a pheasant and they were in serious trouble," blurted Mary. "Are you sure" "Yes mother" Jean thought for a moment "Mary, go and get Hilda and Colin. We'll have to go and see what we can do!" she cried.

When they were all ready the family went to Hamish's house and knocked at the door which was opened by Hamish's younger brother. "Andrew, tell your parents we need to speak with them" said Jean Grant. Agnes McLeod came to the door and invited them in. "The boys have been taken up to the Countess's house; they are supposed to have taken a pheasant," Jean went on to tell them of the circumstances. Archie became very angry, "Who the hell do they think they are taking the lads to the big house; they were only snaring rabbits." Archie ranted. Agnes McLeod glared at her husband; "Archie for goodness sake shouting is no good, we'll have to go and get the boys out of there." "I agree. That's all we can do," said Jean Grant. "Alright, Agnes you better get the children ready, come on the sooner the better," said Archie, trying to get back in control. When everyone was ready they made their way up to the big house to try to get the boys released.

Donald and Hamish had found it very painful being dragged up to the big house by Dewar, they knew that they had done nothing wrong, but it seemed that Dewar was determined to get them up to the house. As they approached the main drive, the head gillie John McDonald appeared. "What's this about?" he asked. "These young thieves stole a pheasant" replied Dewar. McDonald grabbed hold of Hamish, allowing

Dewar to get a better grip of Donald, "We've lost enough birds this year; we'll see what her ladyship says."

The Countess of Badenoch felt that life had cheated her; shortly after she married the Earl he was killed. He had been out riding when his horse slipped as it was picking its way along a narrow path on the hillside, throwing him to the ground, he continued rolling downhill until he struck a tree. When his servants got down to him he was dead. She never got over his death and became very embittered, earning her the reputation of being hard and vindictive.

The boys were frogmarched the rest of the way up the long twisting drive and into the house itself. They stood in the hallway until the Countess appeared. A middle aged lady dressed all in black, "Who are these boys? Why have you brought them here Mr Dewar?" she asked. "They were heading for Strathgowan with rabbits and one of your pheasants Ma'am," The Countess listened to what Dewar said as he described how he had intercepted them but she was watching the boys. She confronted them. "You have stolen my pheasant, you are thieves!" She shouted. "No we didn't! It got caught in a snare it was not our fault," said Donald. Despite the boy's denials she turned to her men and said, "Lock them in the cellar until I decide what to do with them." The two men led the boys down a flight of stone steps and pushed them into a dark storage cupboard locking the door behind them.

Later she came down accompanied by Dewar who was carrying a lantern, she stood looking at the boys, "You stole my pheasant, I will not have that, and then you fought with my men," she said. "We did not fight with them they were hurting us, and we did not steal the bird it got caught in our snare and it was on the other side of the river," blurted Donald. "Do not tell me lies you stole the pheasant and were on your way home with it when Mr Dewar caught you, you are lying," she paused and stared at the boys. "You will stay here till I make up my mind as to what I will do with you. Mr Dewar, leave them some water, but give them no food," she said. Then she and Dewar left with the boys sitting on the stone floor in the dark. "Hamish what is going to happen?" asked Donald. "I don't know, we haven't done anything wrong, but no one seems to believe us," replied Hamish "I think that Dewar and McDonald have been making it up, sooking in with the Countess, and she's believed them," said Donald. "We're better not thinking about it," said Hamish and the boys then lapsed into silence.

At the same time as the Countess was talking to the boys, Jean Grant, Archie and Agnes McLeod had arrived on the forecourt with their children and were met by John McDonald who was not prepared to listen to any excuse. "They are young lads, they set snares, you probably did yourself when you were young, they were just doing what boys do, they weren't trying to steal a pheasant," said Archie, but the gillie would not listen to him. Archie became heated and yelled at the gillie, "Get these lads out here or I'll be in there myself and get them!" "That you will not do!" shouted the gillie back at him "you'll get off these premises or I'll set the hounds on you" "Just try it you bastard!" threatened Archie and made a grab at the gillie, who evaded the lunge and tripped Archie so that he fell at the gillie's feet, McDonald then gave him a hefty kick on the side.

The Countess returned from the cellar and hearing the voices from the forecourt she looked out of the window realising that things were becoming worse, she ordered her servants to go to the front of the building to help the gillie. When Archie fell, the two women and the bigger children ran to help him and were set upon by the servants, who having armed themselves with sticks and clubs began to beat them about the head. Soon all three of the parents and some of the older children were helpless on the ground all of them bruised and wounded by the servants while the younger children screamed and cried. "Now get out of here you lot, you have not heard the last of this." McDonald stood between the big house and the driveway preventing any one from getting to the house. Slowly the dejected families began to make their way down the drive.

Chapter 3

Archie could hear the beat of horse's hooves drumming on the ground outside his home, and the shouting of men. He stirred in his bed and was rising to see what was happening when the door suddenly burst open and a group of policemen entered. They went from room to room shouting, and gathering the family from their beds. "Whit dea ye think yer doin?" shouted Archie. "We're here tae arrest you lot for theft and attacking the Countesses men yer going to court." "We were attacked ye stupid man! Look at us; we've all got bruises, are ye blind? Our son caught a pheasant by mistake and when we went to see about it we were attacked, even the children." "We're only doing whit we were told, get dressed yer comin wi us." He turned to Agnes, "That means you too mistress, get yer young ones together." Archie tried to prevent the police from taking his family but he was outnumbered and eventually the family were rounded up and marched out to the street.

About a hundred yards from the door stood a four-wheeled wagon with closed sides; the man up front was known to Archie as Joseph McPhie and beside him sat Sergeant Wilson of the local police. "Where are we going?" demanded Archie. "What's all this about?" Sergeant Wilson replied, "Yer off to Dalmhore, the sheriff will be seeing you tomorrow so just stay there and keep quiet, your only making things worse for yersel the way yer behaving." Jean Grant and her family were already in the wagon looking shocked and frightened. "The police were at the house before it got light, they forced us out to this wagon, what are they going to do?" she asked Agnes McLeod. Archie said something under his breath which caused Agnes to give him a furious look. The wagon started off with the families being jostled inside as the horses trotted swiftly through the town, Jean Grant held on to the side of the wagon with one hand and tried to hold the younger children with the other. Agnes and Archie were doing the same on the other side of the wagon; they bumped their way across the bridge towards Inchmhor, turning in to the entrance of the estate and up the long twisting drive.

McDonald and Dewar returned to the cellar where they found the boys not only frightened but cold and hungry. "Right you two you're for the high jump." said McDonald. Donald looked frightened and asked, "Where are we going?" "You're for Dalmhore." "What happens in Dalmhore?" "That's where the court sits, and that's where you're going. Come on." The boys were taken to the courtyard where they were roped together and told to stand to await their fate. When the wagon arrived in the courtyard it turned round heading back down the drive. McDonald undid their ropes and pushed them into the back of it like a bundle of rags. The mothers rushed to comfort their sons, but the boys were so shocked that all they could do was cry.

The wagon left the estate and rumbled on although the pace had slowed, until they came to the outskirts of Cairnmhor. Joseph the driver stopped to give the horses a rest and a nose bag of feed. Once the horses were fed he opened the back of the wagon and handed in a jug of broth and some slices of cold porridge; the boys were fed first, then the other children and finally the adults. "Why are we going to Dalmhore when we have done nothing wrong?" Archie asked the sergeant. "Because the sheriff sits at Dalmhore and that's where yer going, ye broke the King's Law, ye stole a pheasant and attacked the Countess's men. God knows whit the sheriff will say." "The old witch up in the big hoose is the one who's guilty, her men attacked us when all we wanted to do was plead for the lads," replied Archie. "Now close yer mouth ye stupid man yer only making it worse for yersel, it's you in the wagon while the granny has her afternoon tea," retorted Wilson. "The witch thinks she's God, no one can do anything or say anything without her having some say in it, a stupid pheasant out of hundreds she breeds and she can do whit she wants." Archie was still angry, his head and ribs were sore from the severe beating he had taken from the servants the night before. The wagon moved on, the relentless juddering of the iron clad wooden wheels finding every stone, every rut, making the journey for the families very uncomfortable as they could feel every uneven spot on the road.

As the wagon continued on its journey, the families were finally beginning to settle down. Hamish and Donald were still very distressed, they were only eleven and apart the broth and porridge they had eaten nothing since the day before. They lay listless on the floor of the wagon for most of the journey, slowly starting to tell their parents about the treatment they had received from the countess and her servants. "They locked us up, then the countess came down and told us we were liars and thieves and that we would be sent away for our wickedness. Mother, we didn't mean to catch a pheasant it was caught in our snare, but she wouldn't listen. Then when you came up to the house one of the servants came in and started shouting and swearing at us. Hamish threw a stool at him and he started to hit us with his fists and kicking us." As Donald was speaking Hamish was rolling up a sleeve to show the black and blue wealds on his skin. "The bastard got his share too," he said. "I got him a beauty with that stool; I bet he has a black eye today." At least there was still a fight in him, but the boys really did not feel quite so brave.

The wagon finally arrived at Dalmhore. They were removed to a cell at the back of the police station which contained a table two chairs and a pile of mattresses in a corner. The two mothers laid out the mattresses and tried to make all the children as comfortable as possible, some of them fell asleep; others sat very still, eyes staring at nothing. They were all wakened from their thoughts by the door suddenly opening and the sergeant appeared with some dried bread and soup by way of a meal. Everyone was hungry but it was the children who were first to be fed, then the adults. After their meagre meal the children again settled down and the three adults had an opportunity to discuss their situation. "The Countess seems to want to get rid of us but I don't know why," said Agnes McLeod. "Well she got rid of most of The Clansmen to make way for all those sheep," replied Archie. "She seems to get a thrill from hurting people; she's a ruthless bitch and no mistake." Jean Grant knew about The Clearances but did not understand them. "Why are they getting rid of The Clans, and what have sheep got to do with it?" "A lot of the Clan Chiefs are driving The Clansmen off their land because sheep gives them more money," explained Archie. Jean sat in silence. "We seem to be joining them," she said with resignation. They settled down for the night, trying to be as comfortable as they could, Donald and Hamish whimpered a bit during the night, but sleep, fitful as it was, finally came. They were wakened at first light, stiff and cold. When the constable opened the door and handed in a meal of cold porridge and water, "You better get yourselves ready you will be up in front of the sheriff as soon as he arrives," he said. Unknown to the families the Countess had sent a letter with the sergeant to be given to the sheriff, supposedly putting her case. In fact it was to remind the sheriff that, as his cousin, she was expecting that he would make an example of these people or the possible future work he would receive from her would be cut back. Sheriff McCall did not like to be put under this kind of pressure, and made up his mind to ignore her comments and treat these people leniently.

About ten thirty the prisoners were called into court and the proceedings were begun. The sergeant told the court of the countess's version of what had happened, but from the start it looked as if the sheriff would dismiss the case. Archie was becoming angry as the sergeant described what had happened and stood up gesticulating at the sheriff. "We were only trying to find out what they were supposed to have done!" he yelled. "Sit down man," said the policeman who was standing in the dock with the families. "Why should I sit down we are innocent, it's the bitch up at Badenoch who should be in here?" cried Archie as he tried to defend the families. "Sit down!" demanded the sheriff. But Archie was in full flow, "I'll not sit down, you are all the same you lot, these boys did nothing wrong and when we try to defend them we end up in the dock, you make me sick." As he finished his tirade the policeman in the dock grabbed him and forced him to sit down. The sheriff had listened to Archie's outburst and despite his earlier views he felt that he had been personally attacked. "It appears that these two boys have inherited the violent and dishonest traits of their parents; you are all sentenced to ten years in the penal colony of Freemantle, Australia!" he said before starting to rise.

The adults were stunned; they were being sent to a foreign land because a stupid pheasant had walked into a rabbit snare. Archie changed colour when he heard the verdict, this could not be true, he had tried to defend his son and as a result they were all being sent to Australia, wherever that was, he had not even heard of the place. "That old bitch did this!" he screamed at the sheriff but the policeman at Archie's side struck him with a baton and Archie fell to the floor of the dock. Agnes ran to his side and the younger children started screaming at the sheriff's receding figure, resulting in the policemen invading the dock and hustling them all into the cell they had left that morning.

After half an hour the sergeant came into the cell and said. "Right yer all for Australia so just make up yer minds to accept it." "Where the hell's Australia?" asked Archie. "What about justice?" "You've seen all the justice you're going to get, you stupid man. I told you to behave but you had to try and out do the sheriff. Now settle down there's nothing you can do now the sheriff has set your sentence, so shut up." With that he disappeared and the group were left to face a very uncertain future.

CHAPTER 4

"Right you lot get yourselves ready you're on your way." They had been held in Dalmhore for three weeks confined to the cells at the rear of the courthouse, fed on cold porridge and the occasional bowl of broth. Archie and the two women gathered the children and led them out to the wagon which was standing at the entrance to the courthouse. The wagon rolled on and on; the driver was again Joseph McPhie who although doing his job was sympathetic to the families. Archie shouted "Joseph where are we going? Why have you come this way?" "We're going to Fort William, that is Loch Laggan over there," Donald glanced out the side of the wagon, to his left he saw a great loch stretched to the horizon, and to the right the mountains rose to meet the sky, he was able to get some idea of where they were going. The journey from Dalmhore was long and uncomfortable; they took turns to lie down on the hard floor of the ever-jolting wagon, the others had to stand or squat. Everyone was feeling the effects of tiredness and lack of decent food. Hamish and Donald were especially upset by their situation, they felt responsible for what had happened, and that everyone had to suffer this journey to somewhere unknown. Archie was also feeling angry and guilty that his outburst had caused this, but he was still telling everyone how he felt at the treatment they had received. "What gave that woman the right to destroy people's lives in this way, on a whim?" He was not now calling her a bitch, and had begun to realise the seriousness of his position. He felt the strain of being the only man and the need to be protective of his charges, he knew his wife Agnes was strong and reliable, his long hours at work meant that she had learned to be, as he was seldom there. His eldest son Hamish was a tough lad, game to try anything and strong, he would be alright; young Andrew was nine but quite well built for his age, and clever. Colin was eight and a bit on the small side, while the two girls Jean aged seven and Fiona five were just too young. Jean Grant, had also shown great stamina during their time together, and then again as a widow she had had to learn to be resilient for the sake of her children. Yes he would be able to rely on her. Donald, whom he knew as Hamish's pal, seemed to be a likely lad, a bit more subdued than Hamish but quite tough and appeared intelligent. The other boy James, the sisters Mary and Hilda were still young and would have to be looked after.

Archie glanced out the side of the wagon and saw tinkers tents, just humps of canvas and branches. The tinkers made their living making and selling clothes pegs and trinkets, they were extremely poor but at least they had their freedom. He was beginning to appreciate the meaning of that evocative word, he was very conscious that they were prisoners, the thought sent shivers down his spine and he could not shake off the feeling of great fear. Donald also realised that he was helpless, he too would stare out the side of the wagon to take his mind off the dreadful situation, and he looked at the passing scenery, he made a mental note of the flowers and the shapes and shadows created by the hills and dips in the track they were following. He tried to memorise the strange shapes outlined by puddles some of which were framed by grass or flowering weeds, and to imagine how the heather looked and the bluebells which could be seen on the lower slopes of the hills. The wagon passed several poor villages and gradually descended. Finally they could see a large stretch of water; Archie shouted to the driver, "Where is this Joseph?" "Fort William," was the reply. Donald was shaken from his dream to face the stark reality of this world. Archie knew of this place with dread; this was the starting point for all those who had been transported during The Great Clearances. Now it was beginning.

CHAPTER 5

The wagon came to a halt on the quayside and the group could see the side of a ship, sails furled and more importantly prisoners similar to themselves filing up the gangway. Joseph herded the families out of the wagon and onto the dockside. "Right over to the gangway and follow these people you see on the dock." The new arrivals looked round at their surroundings and became aware of the houses and the enormous bulk of Ben Nevis behind them. Joseph stood at the bottom of the gangway as his charges were boarding. Archie was last to board and as he passed Joseph put his hand on his shoulder and said, "Good luck to you and your family." Once on board they were shepherded down a hatchway to the lower deck, once all of them were down they heard the hatch slam shut and firmly bolted behind them. "What happens now?" Archie asked one of the other men in their group. "I've no idea," the man replied, "But I don't think you and I are going to be free to go anywhere soon." Sometime after that they felt movement as the ship started to leave the jetty. After a time members of the crew came down with a meal of cold mutton stew washed down with a drink from a water barrel which was the only item of furniture in the place. The food was welcomed by the travellers, as they were all on the point of exhaustion, each having endured similar journeys to those from Strathgowan. Donald felt better once he had eaten, his head began to clear and he realised that he must now try to look after his mother and his brother and sisters.

The captives started talking among themselves and the Grants and McLeod's discovered that there were three other families beside themselves, mostly from the Badenoch region. All had been crofters who had been removed from their homes by the Countess to make way for sheep. Most had done less than Archie and his group, yet they had been told they too were going Australia. After talking to them Archie was able to find the situation more acceptable, there was a comfort in knowing that others were in the same position.

The ship sailed down Loch Linnhe past Seal Island and south past other small islands till they came to a large bay. They entered the harbour at Oban in the small hours of the morning. Somehow the now larger group had found that they had managed to get some sleep or at least rested. They were all wakened at dawn by members of the crew coming down to the hold to give them some breakfast. "When you finish this food you will be leaving this ship and transferred to another, you have five minutes," yelled one of the seamen. The families gulped down their food and were then taken on deck, roped together, marched off the ship and lined up on the quay. Further along the dockside there was a vast pile of cargo ready to be carried aboard a very large sailing clipper ship which would be their transport to Australia. They were made to stand on the jetty for about an hour before being marched aboard SS Vigilant, a three masted schooner. Waiting to greet them was Captain Dunscomb, a Liverpool seaman with a reputation for strict discipline. He was under contract to take prisoners from Britain to Australia, to him they were just cargo and this was a business, he was paid to get them to Australia as soon as possible.

He watched the motley crew come aboard. The new group were lined up on the deck and Captain Dunscomb standing on the quarter deck surveyed his cargo, waiting until everyone was aboard then he addressed them. "You are on this ship as my prisoners. You will be well treated if you obey orders from me and my crew; if you resist any order you will be punished severely, I want that to be clearly understood. Right, Mr Finnegan get the younger children below, the rest back on the jetty and load stores," "Aye, aye sir" responded Finnegan. The younger children were led down to the lower deck where they were allowed to play, knowing the children were safe helped to ease the stress of the others.

Jean Grant, Archie and Agnes and all the other adults were put to work under the supervision of the crew to load the vast cargo of provisions that they had seen stacked up. Hamish and Donald and other older children were also included but were given lighter loads. It was hard work but it meant that they were not so aware of their plight, there were moments when everyone was getting tired and stopped for a break, they were shouted at by the crew. As they were unused to what sort of treatment to expect they observed the rules as best they could. As time passed the huge pile of boxes and sacks grew less until at dusk the exhausted prisoners were marched back on board and were only too glad to receive another meal. Tired as they were, one other thing had to be attended to before they were locked up for the night, hammocks! It was a moment of light relief as they struggled with the strings of this strange contraption. They discovered that there were metal hooks on all the walls-the sailors called them bulkheads-from which to hang the hammock, and with the aid of a blanket they were able to enjoy the most relaxing night's sleep since they were arrested.

At Sunrise they were awakened by whistles and shouts. The peculiar swaying of the deck, "What has happened?" Archie asked one of the seamen who brought them some food, "We've sailed. You better get used to it; we've a long way to go." They were in the open sea. A daily routine was soon established, the male prisoners were put to work on duties on the ship and the women were instructed to do the cooking and looking after the children. The older children were also put to work, Hamish and Donald were called out by Finnegan and given the job of lookout on the upper yard crow's-nest, "Where is the crow's-nest?" asked Hamish. "Up there the small platform at the top of the mast." Said Finnegan pointing upwards both boys looked up and cringed at the thought of being at such a height. They were frightened, but they knew that they could not refuse; they would have to overcome their fear of high places. Hamish was first to go up, after moments of hesitation he managed to reach the crow's-nest and was able to complete his watch, Donald watched him make the climb; he was not as sure as even the thought of climbing the rigging made him nervous. When his turn came he was shown how to clamber outside the ship but doing it was a different matter, he was holding on to the wet ropes, and then had to climb the rigging from the outside till it narrowed into the mast. When he got there he was almost overwhelmed by the tremendous height and the swaying of the ship, this was really terrifying, but he was not finished. He still had to get up and over the yard, steady himself and then a vertical climb until he reached the barrel shaped platform called the crow's-nest. As he climbed the noise of the flapping sails added to the fear he felt and when he did get there he then had to stay for four hours at a stretch.

Donald soon became used to his duty, he accepted that he had no choice and tried to make the best of it. During the day it could be quite pleasant if there were no other ships and nothing but open sea, he could relax and daydream about Scotland, although mostly he just worried about his mother and younger brother and sisters and what the future would bring. Night was different, then he had to deal with high winds, rain or both, the climb was always the same no matter the weather, he remained afraid of the climb both up and down for the entire voyage. Hamish too was apprehensive about the height but he looked on it as a bit of an adventure. In a way he was enjoying the trip as he felt closer to his father who was now starting to behave as a father should. When he was coming off lookout duty he was allowed to chat to his father for a few moments, moments which they were both beginning to cherish. From Archie's point of view, he too was beginning to relax; he did not need to earn money for food that was provided by the ship, as a joiner he was set to work with the shipwright doing work very similar to the work on building sites. During the day he fitted in with the crew but at night he reverted to being in custody and was locked up below decks with his fellow prisoners. The parents and their children gradually got into a routine as the ship sailed south from Oban, passing between the isle of Jura, the Mull of Kintyre and down the west coast until turning east and anchoring in Plymouth Sound.

CHAPTER 6

The Scottish prisoners were locked below decks as the ship approached Plymouth and anchored in the Sound. More criminals were to come on board, they were ferried out to the ship in a large rowing boat their wrists shackled. As the boat reached the gangway they were led one by one up the steps to the main deck where they were lined up. The boat then returned to shore and began to transport more stores to the ship. They sailed on the tide, and as they got out into the English Channel Captain Dunscomb appeared on the quarterdeck and gave these prisoners the same warning he had given the Scottish families then he said "Mr Finnegan get everyone on deck and start getting these stores below," "Aye, Aye capn," responded Finnegan. Heading for the hatchway he herded all the adult prisoners back on deck. "Right you lot these stores have to be put down in the hold. You," he pointed to Archie "starts getting them down, the rest of you follow him." Archie picked up a sack and headed for the hatchway followed by the other convicts. When all the supplies were stored the new prisoners were put down to the deck below the Scottish families, most of the new comers were petty thieves; the dregs of the big cities like London or Birmingham, criminals who had never done a day's work in their lives who lived by their wits. They were now faced with a situation that they did not understand and could not overcome. Captain Dunscomb would see to that. The following morning the ship continued in a southerly direction. The sails full and the rigging straining from a stern wind, the sun rising over a vast ocean, the whistling of the wind, the flapping of the sails and the noise of the crew shouting to each other above the wind, the orders from the boson's mate. The ship was at work. The crew had found the Scottish prisoners easy going and cooperative: they were not to know that they were there as a result of a political situation. The others were criminals and as such they were beginning to show what they were really like. John Carson was a petty thief from Taunton another Devonshire town. He was a small weasel of a man who would be quite happy to kill his granny for the gold in her teeth! He was delegated to assist the sail maker who had told him to get a batch of sail cloth from the sail maker's locker but he did not want to be cooperative, "Get that sailcloth," the order came from Jake Finnegan. "Get the bloody thing yourself!" yelled Carson. Finnegan did nothing. He just walked away from the man then suddenly turned and using a knotted rope end, which he always carried, he struck Carson across the face with such force that he drew blood. Carson fell to the deck in both great pain and shock; he received a kick from the mate as an added punishment. "Don't you ever disobey me again now get that sailcloth," roared Finnegan for all to hear, the rest of the prisoners kept their heads down, Finnegan stood his ground until Carson did as he was ordered, this was not a man to be trifled with.

Once the ship left Plymouth Sound things settled down once again to the daily routine, the weather was fine and Donald and Hamish were even beginning to get used to the climb. It was not long before they were passing round the coast of France and entering the northern most point of the Bay of Biscay. Night was approaching as they entered the bay but before that the swell had already increased and they were finding it difficult to keep their feet on the ever moving deck. Sailing down the coast had been upsetting enough, but now they were to encounter seas they could not previously have imagined. As they sailed further south the waves became higher and the pounding terrified the families. The children were lashed into their hammocks, where despite the swaying they were safe, although that was no guarantee against sickness and the deck was soon covered in vile smelling vomit, which the women tried in vain to clean up. The storm went on for two days until they rounded the northern coast of Spain when the weather returned to a reasonable calm and the women were able to clean up the quarters. During the stormy days in the bay Donald and Hamish had to continue to do the watches in the crow's-nest and these Donald found really terrifying, when he did get up the mast he could see very little but he had to be there as protection for the ship in case there were any other ships around.

Other prisoners tried at times to get the better of the crew, but none succeeded, and John Dunscomb being an astute captain, was only using the criminal prisoners in small groups, most of the time they were locked up below decks and only allowed up on deck to carry out ships duties five or six at a time, they had to work with the crew so that he had control at all times. Archie was different, as a trained joiner he was allowed to continue to help the shipwright who had lots of work to do as the stormy passage through the bay had caused a great deal of damage. He had been accepted by the crew and was allowed some privileges making life a bit easier for the two families from Strathgowan. One of the privileges that resulted was that the Scottish prisoners were permitted more freedom than would normally be given, they were also given extra food and the fittings on their deck were made a little more comfortable especially for the children. Jean Grant and Agnes McLeod had now become good friends and shared their fears and dreams, both were afraid for their children especially the two older boys. They were not stupid and the thought of Donald and Hamish climbing to the crow's-nest two or three times a day gave them almost as much fear as the boys themselves.

As time went on the two women were starting to be noticed by some of the crew, who knew that Agnes was the wife of the prisoner who was helping the shipwright, but Jean Grant appeared to be unattached and attracting the interest of one particular seaman called George Poole. Poole had been brought up on a farm in Dorset and had decided that there was a world out there, he had signed on as a seaman for the duration of the voyage, he had no idea that he would be on a prison ship, but he was prepared to make the best of it. At twenty-five he was ten years younger than Jean and she found it quite flattering that this young sailor should be interested in her. Had she been in Scotland, as a widow, it would not have been seemly to be seen with another man but the situation she was now in seemed to make it acceptable. "Jean, I'm not sure. These men are rough seamen; getting involved with one of them might cause trouble." Agnes was afraid for her friend. Fearing that females among a group of seamen might bring trouble, she advised Jean to take care and not to lead the man on. "I know Agnes but it is nice that this young man wants to talk to us especially as he's so attractive? What harm can it do? He won't become a prisoner in Australia," was Jean's response.

The weather was getting warmer, they had been at sea for about two weeks and gradually the temperature was rising, gone were the dark cold nights of the Bay of Biscay, now it was hot from morning till night. The ship had hugged the shore for some days, passing down the coast of Spain and Portugal, where it was stopped and papers examined before being allowed to proceed. They now appeared to be travelling east instead of south, and were getting closer to the shore that could faintly be seen on the horizon. Although it was warm, dark clouds were gathering, and the crew were starting to lash down everything that might move, obviously thinking that there was a storm coming. As normal when the weather was stormy the crew had to reduce the amount of sail and they were all over the rigging reefing in the sails. Donald was assigned the crow's-nest as lookout. He hated being up there in a storm but he had no choice; he knew that if he refused he would be locked up below with bread and water, if anyone remembered to feed him. He had been told that on one occasion when they were busy the seamen had forgotten a prisoner for two days leaving him without food or water, the poor man was delirious by the time they got back to him. He made his way up the mast with a heavy heart, the rigging was already wet from the spray whipped up by an ever-increasing wind, he could feel the ropes slipping through his fingers as he climbed and the ship seemed to be bobbing around like a cork. He was terrified. Finally he reached the relative safety of the crow's-nest, he looked around and tried to settle, there was little he could see, as far as the horizon there were huge white topped waves with a large black canopy of sky, and things did not look good.

Down below the rest of his family and all the other prisoners were put below decks, the children as always were in their hammocks, and on deck the crew fought to try and keep the ship on course. The storm raged for a long time, occasionally Donald got a glimpse of the coast, was it his imagination or was the shoreline getting closer? The ship was dipping and rolling in the violent waters. Suddenly it gave a lurch forward and seemed to dip into the sea, he held on for dear life as the mast swayed forward and the bows of the vessel disappeared for a moment below the mighty waves. As quick as the bow disappeared below the waves it recoiled and he found himself hanging on for grim death. This swaying sensation continued for a time, he realised that it might damage the ship and if it did then he was in the wrong place, he decided that he had to get down or he would be killed, he would have to get over the rail of the crow's-nest and endeavoured to get down the wet and moving rigging. Very gingerly he started to climb over but as he did his foot slipped between the strands of the rigging; he was caught. At the same time there was a loud crack and he was thrown backwards as the mast snapped in the middle!

CHAPTER 7

Donald was cold and wet, he was aware of being in water and his foot hurt, he could not understand what had happened, he realised that his foot was still trapped in the rigging and what remained of the mast. The ship itself looked a wreck; the remainder of the mast and rigging were draped over the stern and were dragging the ship down. As he was still attached Donald being trailed behind what remained of the ship, which was being tossed about in the continuing storm. He drifted in and out of consciousness, each time he could see the hull of the ship before him but it appeared lower in the water, he was watching the demise of a ship, and he was afraid that this could be his death too. Donald was aware that the sun was shining, he had no idea of time, and he was still in the water although by now it was calm. In front of him the remains of the ship were propped up on rocks at an awkward angle and on board were a group of people staring down at him. Through a great hole in the ship's side the water flowed in and out and there were barrels and other flotsam canvas bundles floating inside the hull.

A boat appeared from behind the rocks and made its way towards him. He had no idea who they were, but when the men in the boat got to him they cut the rigging which had held him to the ship, and very gently lifted him into their boat. He must have passed out when he was freed from his wet prison, now he found himself in a warm bed, there were voices in the distance which he could not understand. A lady came into the room dressed all in white with a high stiff headdress. She spoke in a strange language and began to spoon-feed him with some kind of soup. It tasted funny, but it was warm and he took all that she had in the bowl. She said something that he did not understand then disappeared only to return with a second bowl this time of stewed meat, which she again fed to him. After he had eaten she left the room and quietly closed the door, he was comfortable in a warm bed, and was soon overcome by sleep. When he woke, he was not sure what time of day it was, where he was or what had happened to the rest of the people on the ship. The skin of his face, hands and arms felt very hot and stung like nettle stings. His foot felt sore. He rose and limped across the tiled floor which felt cool to his bare feet before opening the door and glancing outside.

He was in a wide corridor with bright white walls and reddish tiles on the floor. He looked both ways but there was no sign of life. He closed the door again and crossed the room to a glass door which led out into a garden. The sun was shining and it was hot, he was not used to sun like this, there were funny looking trees that he had never seen before. He was startled to hear voices and returned to the room just as the door opened. There was Poole the seaman who had befriended his mother. Following George was indeed his mother, his brother James and his sisters Mary and Hilda. He was sure he was dreaming. They were wearing strange clothes and were laughing and excited. They looked happier than he had seen them these last few weeks, and appeared quite at home in this strange place. Jean Grant came forward first and hugged him tightly, "Donald! We thought you had died in the sea, thank God you are safe, are you hurt?" He could not reply as she was holding him so close, he felt as if she had squeezed all the air out of him. Mary and Hilda then came forward and kissed him lightly on the forehead. James stood back and did not make the same show of affection but Donald could tell by his beaming smile he was glad to see his brother. When he had recovered after this shock, they helped him along the corridor to a large room. His mother was very concerned about his foot, but he assured her it was not too sore and he was alright. He was offered a drink which he had never tasted before; orange in colour and with a strange taste but it was very nice. Jean Grant then started to tell him what had happened, "When the mast broke the ship drifted until it hit some rocks; we did not know what had happened to you. We heard the bang when it snapped but we had no idea what had caused it, we were alright as the ship seemed to settle and our deck was above water level. I don't think the English prisoners who were below us survived." Poole then broke in, "The ship started to founder, but we were near the shore and the crew managed to get the boats free and get to land. They were more interested in saving themselves and ignored the prisoners. Everyone thought that you were lost when the mast came down." Jean Grant then took up the story again, "We were on the first deck and clear of the water, the poor men on the deck below had no chance. We were frightened because we were locked in but luckily the local fishermen had come out to the wreck to try to salvage what they could and found us. They let us out and brought us ashore the nuns here have been wonderful and given us food and shelter." "How did I get here?" asked Donald. "The fishermen had returned to the ship to resume their search and they found you hanging over the remains of the mast. They had seen you from the deck and sent a boat for you, they brought you here to this convent and you had slept for two days," replied Poole. Donald nodded although he still felt very weak but he was delighted to see his family again.

Donald looked round the room his family had been given. There were three beds, a small table with a bowl and a jug of water and the same glass doors as the room he had been in, and outside the beautiful gardens he had seen earlier. His mother looked younger and more relaxed than he could remember. His brother and sisters were obviously happy; they appeared to be enjoying their freedom and now that he had come back from the dead they were overjoyed as they had thought that they had lost him in the shipwreck. There was a knock at the door and in came Hamish, "Donald! It's great to see you! We all thought you had fallen overboard," he cried. He was followed by his family; they too had the appearance of being relaxed and happy, even Archie looked pleased to see that his son's pal was back with them. After settling down on one of the beds Donald curious to fill in gaps started to ask questions, "What happened to the captain and all the men?" he asked. George Poole said, "When the ship hit the rocks the crew were all on the upper deck, we launched the boats and rowed for shore, but the tide was against us and we ended up about three miles down the coast. A short time later I saw you all being rescued up here, and decided to come and see if there was anything I could do. I was worried that your mother might be in great danger." Poole appeared sincere in his concern mainly for Jean Grant but also for the others. "In fact you are better off here than we were, the local fishermen are very kind but they do not have much for themselves let alone a ship's crew," he continued. "Where are we? Where is this place?" "It's called Rota, we're near a town called Cadiz, and we are in Spain."

Donald had no idea where Spain was but the he liked the sound of the place. The two families were obviously content to be here. "Are the other people here too?" asked Donald. "I mean the people we met on the ship." "Yes, they all have rooms along the corridor." The nuns, for that was what the strangely dressed ladies were, had looked after all the families very well and they were all settled down to an unexpected freedom. The Captain and his men came to the convent with the intention of arresting the missing prisoners, but the Mother Superior would not allow them to be taken and said that they were guests and the Captain had no authority in Spain. Captain Dunscomb threatened the Mother Superior with the might of the British navy, but Mother Gabriel was not to be moved. Eventually the captain gave up; in the end he returned to England with his crew but without his captives, he told the inquiry that all his charges had drowned, knowing the conditions on prison transport ships no one doubted his

CHAPTER 8

After three months everyone was beginning to settle down in their new land, they had left the convent with grateful thanks to the nuns.

Hamish and his family had found accommodation in the village. Archie managed to get a job with a local man making guitars; a musical instrument unknown to the small contingent from Scotland. There was also a great deal of furniture making in the area so with his experience he was able to fit in. Hamish, Donald and the other children were attending school having been accepted by the local children, they were already able to speak some Spanish with them. Mr Poole or George as he was now known seemed to be genuinely fond of Jean Grant and it was becoming obvious that she liked him; he had decided to throw in his lot with her and had not returned to England with the ship's crew. He had managed to get a job with a local farmer which came with a fairly large house. As a result he was able to invite the Grant family to move in with him, James and Donald had one small room and the two girls shared with their mother, George had his own room, and there was a large living space for them all to use. He was now providing the food for the table. The farmer was finding George a good worker and had shown him how to attend to the cork trees and the orange groves. His previous farming experience meant that he did not require supervision and he was becoming a trusted worker.

Six months later as the boys were leaving school for the day, Hamish said "Donald I'm getting a job with Hamidi the mason," Hamish was very excited. "What do you mean a job? You're too young to get a job," replied Donald. "Well I'm to work with him as a messenger for a while," said Hamish. "You're lucky, I wish I could," said Donald. "I have been looking for something to do but I haven't found anything yet." Having been used to helping to provide for his family Donald found time hanging heavy on his hands. Donald could not help but compare Spain with his homeland. In Scotland the sky was usually grey with a lot of rain and snow in the winter and everything from trees to grass a lovely green. Here in Spain the sun shone nearly every day, the wind when it blew was usually warm, the soil a dusty brown and the rocks usually whitish; trees and grass were green but much paler than Donald had been used to. Once a week George would go to market with the farmer to a southern city called Cadiz. One day he suggested to Donald that perhaps he would like to go with them. "I would love to! I have never been to a big town that would be great, thank you." So they arranged that the next time George and the farmer went to Cadiz they would take Donald. While George was at the market Donald walked round the town. He thought that Cadiz was amazing; the sea front with its wide white beaches and the great sea wall in the town itself, up until that time the only town Donald had known was Strathgowan. He also found the number of people surprising, coming from a small town in the Highlands of Scotland he was not used to crowds, here the streets buzzed with the flow of pedestrians going about their business.

Not long after his visit to Cadiz, Donald found out that a local blacksmith called Carlos was looking for a boy to do odd jobs. Carlos made wrought iron fences and intricate gates as well as sword decoration. Donald went to see him asking if he could have a job and he was pleased to be taken on; Carlos also took on a local boy called Pepi. It was hard, heavy work but the thing that fascinated Donald was the way the smith made oriental metal decoration for gates and even finer work for sword scabbards; he could make the scrolls and designs very small. Hamish was enjoying working with the local mason. Both of the boys were learning to be independent and the basics of a trade; there seemed to be little time for childish games now, Hamish did not come to the house so much now but they were still friendly just not as close as they had been. The difference in their interests was now quite wide; Hamish was learning to be what he always wanted to be, a mason. Though still very young he was working with the men on the building sites, he was only a message boy but he was in the trade where he wanted to be. Donald had not exactly planned to be a blacksmith but he had a job and was helping to provide for his family. Pepi had shown that he was not interested in the fine work so the training took two directions. Pepi did the heavy work on gates and railings; Carlos could see the artistic streak in Donald entrusted him with some of the finer detail. After a few months working with Carlos, Donald was starting to learn some of the tricks of working hot metals. Soon he was able to make little trinkets of his own, at first they were very rough but the longer he was there the more he learned. Carlos was a great teacher. Some of the pieces Donald made he was allowed to keep. He took them home for his mother to see; George said they were very good but that he should continue trying to improve them. As time went on and the quality of the trinkets improved George suggested that Donald should try to sell them. Donald was flattered by the suggestion, so the next time George went to the market in Cadiz he took some of the small pieces Donald had made, if they sold that would be marvellous. Donald anxiously waited for George's return. Would they sell and if they did how much money would they make? When George returned he pretended to Donald that nothing had sold, "I'm sorry Donald the people on the market thought I was joking trying to sell bits of iron," as he spoke George winked at Jean then he relented and said, "Donald I sold thirteen pieces. You gave me twenty." He handed Donald a bag. "Here's the money and the ones that did not sell, make some more and I'll take them the next time I go there."

Donald was absolutely delighted! He gave a quarter of the money to George and bought a small present for his mother. This had given Donald an idea; he was working now and had some money of his own. The next time George went to Cadiz he gave him some more knick-knacks he had made. He also asked him to get some pencils and paper, he had been making these items from Spanish designs Carlos had shown him. What if he made up designs of his own? George brought back a slate mounted in wood and a box of slate pencils, he said, "We'll see what you can do, when you have made your drawing, you can wipe the slate clean and start again, and it will be good for you to practice on." Donald could not wait to get started and sat down immediately to try and put down the thoughts he had for the last few months. He tried to draw the bluebells and the other flowers he remembered from Strathgowan, he was a little rusty to start with, but over a couple of weeks he gradually improved and was able to get a reasonable likeness to the plants and flowers he had known. His mother and George were pleased with his start and encouraged him to practice as much as possible, even with the slate they could see that he was able to design small items to make in his spare time after work. Carlos was becoming interested in what Donald was trying to do and allowed him to keep some of the scraps of metal from the main work they did. Donald appreciated this and when he had made more of these small pieces George would take them to market the next time he went. He found that they still sold well; in fact an elderly gentleman had asked if he could order a pair of bookends with a floral decoration. This was a challenge. Donald first set about drawing the design for a thistle, the national emblem of Scotland; he tried to see if he could give it the style that the Spanish were able to do with their flowers. After several attempts he managed to create a stylised thistle, but when he tried to copy it in reverse he found that he had to draw it over and over until he was satisfied. When he tried to make it in metal the results were quite pleasing, he made one facing to the right and one facing left for the bookends and was satisfied with the result. Hamish's father Archie made the wooden frame for the bookends and also a plinth for a third thistle which Donald painted in the bright colours which he Spanish people favoured. George took them to Cadiz market; the old gentleman was delighted with his order. George also sold other pieces but the coloured thistle ornament sold for twice the price of the others. From then on Donald drew all his designs first.

One day his mother said, "Donald you will soon be thirteen, we are going to have a party. They do that here so we might as well have one for you. We will invite Hamish's Mum and Dad, the children and some of the other families. Would you like that? "Yes Mother, that would be wonderful," replied Donald. On the day of Donald's birthday Hamish and his family, and the other people who had been rescued with them, were at the house for tapas. Wine for the adults and, and orange drinks for all the children, it was a pleasant afternoon in the sun. Archie brought his boss who was an expert guitar player so they had music to add to the food and drink. Some of the local children who had become friends, began to dance to the music; a strange heel tapping dance, not unlike the dancing from their native Scotland. Jean Grant and Agnes McLeod watched their families enjoying themselves. So much had happened in the last few months, Hamish and Donald had set off a series of events that neither of them could have imagined. Here they were after this short time living in Spain, sitting in the sun drinking orange juice and wine and fitting in well with their Spanish neighbours. After a few glasses of wine Archie decided to give the locals something to remember and sang a well-known Scottish ballad, he was having fun and the terrors of recent times were in the past. Agnes too was more relaxed, she watched her husband sing and tried to recall the last time she had seen him looking so happy. Since the night they had gone to the Countesses house their life had taken an unexpected twist. The Scottish families and their Spanish friends enjoyed the happy atmosphere and the children were obviously enjoying themselves, the noise from the yard outside told her that. James, Donald's brother was getting bigger, he was nine now. He and his two sisters Mary and Hilda together with Andrew, Colin, and Fiona McLeod were all being taught at the local school, the teacher spoke in Spanish and they were all beginning to speak the language quite well, as could be heard by their chatter in the local dialect.

CHAPTER 9

Five years had come and gone. The families had settled down, winter in Spain was different to back home, wet and windy but never as cold as it had been in Scotland. Donald was not yet considered a tradesman blacksmith, but he had been found to be reliable and was left on his own to deal with jobs, physically he had become a tall, well-built young man and able to deal with the heaviest of work. The summers were very hot and he sometimes found it quite exhausting if they had a big job in the forge, the heat outside and the fire which had always to be kept fully alight made working with the hot metal a sweaty operation. The small items he had started making were still selling well. Each time George took them to the market in Cadiz Donald would replace them, always adding a new design or a new colour because the coloured ones were becoming very popular. There were some regular customers who would order special items, and some of these started to ask for gold inlay. He had no idea how to do this but Carlos suggested a goldsmith called Enrico in Cadiz and the next time George went to the market Donald went with him. Donald stood outside the shop and wondered if he should go in. He was good at his job, the designs and making of the trinkets were his pride and joy, this was what he wanted, this is why he was here; he braced himself and opened the door. The plush interior of the shop was even more daunting. A young man came forward and asked Donald if he could help, "Could I speak to Signor Enrico please?" The young man looked at this boy with the paper parcel, frowned but said nothing and disappeared through a door at the rear. Signor Enrico came into the showroom. "Yes young man how I can help you?" "Thank you for seeing me Signor, you were recommended to me, I was told that you could advise me with a problem I have." Donald went on to explain the reason for his visit and laid out the items for inspection. Enrico looked at the work Donald had brought to him. He studied them carefully nodding as he did, then he said. "Come with me young man." He led Donald through a door and up a flight of stairs. At the top they entered a workshop where a man wearing a white apron was bent over a bench. "Cristian is our designer if you watch him now he can show you what to do. Cristian, this is Donald from Rota could you show him how he could gild these ornaments please?" Signor Enrico then left them. Cristian showed Donald how he could add the gilding to one of the pieces Donald had brought; he also gave him the necessary gilding material for him to take home with him. When he returned to the showroom Signor Enrico said, "Now young man go and try doing what you have been shown, then bring them back for me to see. If the results are good I will display them in the window." Donald was overwhelmed by this offer and agreed that if it worked out he would be back to see him in a month.

When he returned to the village he told his mother of his visit and the offer he had been given, "The man took me to his workshop and Cristian the designer showed me what to do." "Donald you have done well, you are making us so proud! I hope that you keep on doing your best and you will succeed." Later he sat down with slate and pencil to design a range of gifts that would suit an uptown goldsmith. Again he tried to convert one of the Scottish flowers giving it a Spanish twist, he created the pieces and then he tried to gild them. After some experimentation he gradually began to get it right, His mother was his best critic and she said that his memory of the Scottish bluebell was very good but that he should use more gold with the iron. He valued his mother's opinion so he tried adding more, the outcome was good so if it worked with one piece he would try it with the others. The result was the entire collection was beginning to look more gold than iron.

When he walked into the shop with his bundles Signor Enrico said "Well young man how did you get on? Let us see what you have produced." Donald laid out two or three of the pieces he had made on the counter. Signor Enrico stood back to study the collection, then he picked up each piece inspecting the details closely. "First class!" he said, "Let's see them all." The rest of the pieces were lined up and it was evident that he liked what he was seeing. Suddenly he said, "Come and work for me." The implication of what he had said took time to sink in, but when it did Donald tried to be cautious, "What do you want me to do." He asked "Work in the workshops of course, as a trainee goldsmith and designer." Donald was overwhelmed by the offer. When he reached home he told his mother what Signor Enrico had said, "What do you think mother "he asked, "Will you be able to manage?" His mother replied, "Don't worry about us Donald you seem to have a great talent we want you to succeed. We will be alright George and I are planning to marry soon, so you go on, I know this is what you have always wanted. Grab it with both hands, and don't worry about us." Her reassurance, plus the news that she was going to marry George, he had for the last few years really been part of the family, this news left him feeling on top of the world. Now that he had the approval of his mother he could accept Signor Enrico's offer, he had hesitated at first but after persuasion had said that he would think about it.

CHAPTER 10

The move to Cadiz was difficult; this was the first time the family had been split up since their unexpected arrival in Spain. At seventeen Donald looked on it as a good prospect and decided he had to make the most of it, he knew he would miss his family and Hamish, this was an opportunity he could not afford to miss, having been an apprentice blacksmith he was strong, and he was not stupid, he knew he would be alright. Signor Enrico lived not far from his shop. There were rooms above the workshops which were accessible by an outside stair and he offered Donald the use of one of them, the other rooms were occupied by three apprentices. Ramon, Cristian's assistant the young goldsmith who had shown him the gilding methods on his first visit, Pedro, who was learning to be a silversmith and Lorenzo who he had also met on his first visit and who was an apprentice salesman. All were typically Spanish with dark swarthy looks and jet-black hair. Ramon was small in stature and very slim, while Pedro was heavy built and he tended to scowl a lot, Lorenzo was tall and well built and was always very smartly dressed. They welcomed him to the apartment and showed him around pointing out the kitchen and advising him of the various rules they had to live by. He also met Cristian the jewellery designer again, who advised him to find a dealer and get a supply of the right type of paper and art pencils he would require. He found one some streets away, and duly stocked up on the items he needed. He soon settled down to a new life with his work mates, he didn't have a problem at work but and in the apartment his new house mates were inclined to look on him as a workaholic, and were soon making things uncomfortable. Pedro was the worst, being the heaviest he thought that he could bully the others, Donald may have been considered a swot but he didn't feel that he had to give in to this lad. One day he was in his room trying out some new designs when Pedro came in and stood behind him watching him draw, "What do you call that scribble?" he said. Donald ignored him and continued drawing, again he said, "What a mess, are you expecting a smith to be able to copy that?" Having been through a shipwreck and a deportation for catching a pheasant which of course Pedro knew nothing about, and having spent five years as a blacksmith, he was not going to be put upon by a loud-mouth youth. He jumped up and grabbing Pedro by the shirt and said, "Get out of this room you stupid bugger! If I decide to make a design then it has nothing to do with you." He tightened his grip on the big lad "It's none of your business so keep your comments to yourself."

Donald had no trouble after that Pedro avoided him, and he avoided Pedro. The other lads knew what Pedro was like and the confrontation raised his standing with them. Slowly he settled down and began to learn how to work with precious metals and design jewellery. Most of the work he was given in the beginning was the manufacture of Toledo jewellery with its intricate pattern and combination of metals, but he was also encouraged to try out some pieces of his own. Time went quickly, he was learning about the differences in working in gold and silver as opposed to poor old iron, there were similarities and he was able to bring some of the techniques of the blacksmith to bear in his work. His great interest in design and drawing was being encouraged for the first time. He was beginning to get good results and Signor Enrico was pleased as the pieces he was creating were selling quite well. His life was not confined to his work and lodgings.

He got to know a number of people from outside his immediate circle; they would meet in the café's in the evening for a glass of wine. During a conversation one evening the talk got round to horse riding. A young friend called Felipe suggested that he might like to try it, and arranged to meet him in the local park so that they would see how he liked it. One day while still a novice, he was trotting his horse with Felipe, when a very attractive young lady passed, riding side saddle coming from the opposite direction. She was with an older woman who was also riding side saddle and looking very uncomfortable. "Hello Maria, how are you today?" said Felipe. "Very well thank you Felipe," she replied. "This is Donald," he said laughing. "He is still a bit of a novice." "How nice to meet you Donald, don't worry, we were all novices once, pay no attention to Felipe." Donald was enjoying the exercise and continued to ride when he had the opportunity. Very often he would see Maria and her chaperone, after a time the two became friends and would ride together as often as possible. One day while they were riding in the park Donald said, "Maria would you like to walk with me on Sunday afternoon?" Maria was surprised by the question, "Why Donald? I don't know. Yes I would enjoy that, but I would require to have permission from my father and my aunt would probably have to come along, I'm afraid." "That is wonderful Maria. I will be riding here on Friday perhaps you could let me know then." "Yes I could do that Donald." They continued their ride but inside Donald was feeling very elated. The following Sunday the two were strolling through the park and as always there was a solitary figure at a discreet distance behind. Maria's elderly aunt as chaperone. For fun they would often run ahead and hide in the bushes, leaving her aunt searching everywhere; it was more as a tease than a chance to be alone. The two were growing closer and one afternoon as they walked in the park Maria said, "Donald my father has become very curious about you, and would like you to visit with us next Sunday?" "I would be delighted to Maria. Would you please thank your parents for their invitation?"

Signor Del Paco was a small man with a very smart moustache and goatee beard. He was a saddler with a shop near the city boundary. Señorita Del Paco was slightly taller than her husband emphasised by her black hair piled high on her head, held in place by a large lavishly decorated comb. Their home was typical of the region with the house wrapping itself around an open courtyard, and a small garden in the centre. As Donald entered Maria introduced him, "Mother, Father this is Donald. He works for Signor Enrico as a jeweller and designer." "I am pleased to meet you. Maria has told me all about you, thank you for inviting me," said Donald. "Welcome Donnal," Pedro Del Paco said, unable to correctly pronounce his name. "Please feel at home, Maria speaks highly of you," he continued, as he ushered Donald to a large sofa. The family were friendly towards him but he could feel the reserve; no doubt they were wondering who this upstart from Scotland was? True, he was working for a well-known jeweller, respected not only for his upmarket shop but because Signor Enrico was a figure of importance in Cadiz. They were interested in what he did as a jewellery designer, although he did not think they fully understood what was involved. His first visit was fairly short, but as they got to know him the atmosphere gradually improved, eventually to the point of a reluctant acceptance. Donald and Maria continued to go horse riding and he was becoming more proficient as time went on, they used to go to the local beach and race each other through the surf.

He had been so involved with his training and his relationship with Marie that he was surprised to find that Hamish was now married, and was living in the suburbs of Cadiz. Donald took Maria to meet him and his new wife Annetta in their home and was impressed by the style of the house. It was obvious that Hamish was doing well in his chosen profession; the house was well furnished and they were both dressed in the latest fashion. Although Hamish was still the rough diamond he had always been. They met them often after that and Maria and Annetta became good friends. Maria even persuaded Annetta to take up horse riding with them. Hamish had other ideas and kept his feet on the ground. One morning Ramon the young goldsmith shouted, "Donald there's a letter for you! Donald had always kept in touch with his mother and had told her about Maria, this letter was from George to tell him that he and his mother Jean were getting married. He spoke to Maria and her parents who agreed that Maria could go to the wedding with him provided that the aunt went as well as chaperone. He was able to get some time off and when the time came all three made the journey to Rota, the place he now called home. Hamish and Annetta had travelled with them to the village, where they were reunited with his mother and father and all his brothers and sisters.

His family gave them a wonderful welcome. Jean and George had been friends since the voyage and the family were pleased to see them both so happy. The priest, who had known them since their arrival at the convent, married them in the chapel amid the beautifully ornamented shrines which ran up both sides of the very highly decorated building. Jean Grant looked very beautiful in her Spanish wedding dress, no doubt very different from her wedding to his father which had been a poor affair; there had been no money for fancy weddings in the north of Scotland in 1855. Mrs Poole, as she was now, spoke with Maria, she seemed pleased that Donald had found a nice friend, and hoped to see more of her.

A wedding is a great time to meet family and old friends. James now seventeen and the two girls were doing their best to look grown up. The wedding was a great success, his mother looked so happy in the sunshine; they all had a wonderful party with a mixture of Spanish and Scottish music and dance.

CHAPTER 11

Work in the shop was going well. Donald was now working with the chief designer and they were producing some beautiful pieces, which in turn were bringing more people to the shop, Signor Enrico was delighted that his customers were increasing and the income from the new designs was making him a rich man. In return Donald's wage reflected the success, now he felt that he had a career in jewellery design. He had been careful and still had the money from the sale of the iron items he felt financially secure enough to rent a small house near Hamish. He and Marie were out walking when he proposed to her; as was the custom he had already asked her father for permission. They were on the promenade overlooking the sea, the sun was shining the sea was calm-calmer that he was he could feel his legs shaking and his voice trembled a bit. They stopped to sit on the sea wall; he felt that this was the right time and place.

"Maria," he said, "I have something to ask you?" Maria turned and looked him straight in the eye, which he found even more disturbing. He pressed on. "Would you consider becoming my wife?" He held his breath not being sure of the answer he might receive, "I have been waiting for you to ask," she replied. "I would love to be your wife Donald, nothing would please me more." He kissed her tenderly, now he could offer her a ring fit for a designer's wife. It was a fine cluster of diamonds with small amethysts between each diamond. A year later they were married in Cadiz Cathedral, followed by a party in the top hotel in the middle of the city, hosted by Signor Del Paco. Maria's entire family, from her youngest sister to her eighty year old grandmother were there. So too were Jean, now Mrs Poole, and her new husband George, together with James and the girls. Archie and Agnes and their children were also there, so were Hamish and Annetta. Signor Enrico too was invited and he came with his wife, Donald felt that it was the happiest day he had ever known. He and Maria settled down to a domestic life in Cadiz. His work was progressing and customers in the shop were asking for him when they wanted special items as gifts or love tokens.

Setting up home was a new experience for Maria. Donald already had his rented flat but they decided to buy a house near the centre of the city, and she now enjoyed the chance to furnish a home for them both. They spent the first summer after their wedding enjoying married life spending weekends with Hamish and Annetta, and horse riding on the sands. They visited his mother and George and caught up with his brother and sisters, who had now blended in with the locals and were more Spanish than Scottish. Looking back Donald was able to say that this was a particularly happy time. His career too was doing well. Cristian had retired and he had been made head designer by Signor Enrico. He was respected by all the staff in the shop and workshop, including Pedro, the now corpulent silversmith. They talked often of having children and one day when Donald returned from the workshop she asked him to help her with some plans for the extra bedroom they had, "I thought we could decorate in a nice bright colour, perhaps the corner would be a nice sunny spot for the cot." Donald nodded absent-mindedly then realised what she had just said, "Do you mean what I think you mean? Are you going to have a baby?" he was 0verwhelmed by the news and rushed to pick her up swirling her around in a full circle. Donald was thrilled and at the first opportunity he took Maria to visit his mother to inform her that she was to be a Grandmother. Jean Poole was delighted when she was told and gave her daughter in-law a hug as if to say you are now a fully-fledged member of the Grant family.

Donald and Maria returned to Cadiz and went through a period of great happiness waiting for the birth of their first child. Not only that but his work at the shop was being rewarded by orders from other cities in Spain and his name was beginning to be known. He was very content with his lot and the lingering thoughts of Scotland and his home town were pushed to the back of his mind. He would never forget that he was a Scot, but also he was in reality a wanted man. He was not even sure that the Countess was still alive and if she was, would she be aware that he was not only a free man? But that he was a highly talented jewellery designer in the Spanish city of Cadiz. He was becoming a relatively rich man who now owned a house and was even in a position to employ a maid called Elena. The following few months passed with the two of them very happy and looking forward to the coming event. Maria was generally keeping well, but there were signs of a problem, when on an odd occasion she would stagger before regaining her balance. This worried Donald but he did not want to make too much of a fuss about it, he talked to Elena about his concern and asked her to keep a special watch over her mistress. One afternoon while he was busy in his workshop, Signor Enrico came to the door and signalled for him to come outside. Donald left his client and stepped out to the hallway beyond. Signor Enrico was agitated and told Donald that he would have to go home immediately as Maria had had an accident. Donald turned white at the news and rushed home to be met at the door by his mother-in-law, who tried to stop him from entering the lounge, "Donald! Please don't go in!" Brushing past her he saw his wife lying on the sofa, her skin the colour of marble. Donald threw himself at her feet and wept.

The day before the funeral Donald sat with Maria's mother, she was still distressed but was trying to explain to him what had happened. "Maria came to visit with me and we went shopping together. We returned to your house and when we went in Maria said that she was going upstairs to change out of her street clothes. She had only climbed a few steps when she fell backwards hitting her head on the bottom step." She paused "Nothing Elena or I did made any difference and when the doctor finally arrived he told us that Maria was dead, there was nothing we could do." By the time she finished speaking she was in tears. Donald was at a loss. His life had centred on Maria and the child they were to have; now there was nothing. He had been brought to low ebb by the turn of events and spoke to no one for days. He took time off work and returned to Rota to see his mother and step-father where he relaxed a bit. He did a lot of walking and thinking and swung between moods of melancholy and trying to plan for his future. By the end of a week he had made up his mind. He returned to Cadiz and to his studio where he informed his employer that he would be completing the outstanding orders. Then he was going to leave-for

CHAPTER 12

Donald had said his goodbyes to the family when he was at Rota. His mother was very upset about his decision but understood why he was going. She knew how devoted he had been to Maria and how living in the same house, in the same town, would always have memories for him, which at the moment he did not want to face. After returning to Cadiz he had called on Hamish who wished him well, "I'm sorry you have decided to travel you always said you would like to go to America, now you will be able to achieve your goal. I don't think I would like to head there but one day I'd like to return to Scotland." They both laughed at that each thought that it would be impossible but they hoped. "How are you getting there." asked Hamish. "I sail to New York a week on Wednesday from the harbour here in Cadiz." "What are you going to do about money, Pesetas? They won't be any good to you there." "Well I'm in the gold business. I'm going to take gold coins; they trade anywhere." Hamish gave Donald a knowing look, "Good idea." He decided to visit his in-laws and said his farewells. They too understood his reasons for leaving, and thanked him for making their daughters last few years, as his wife, a happy time. He also called in at the studio and said goodbye to his friends there, even getting a farewell hug from Pedro. Now that he had made up his mind Donald was making sure that he attended to everything. He had his tickets for the steamship Picardie. On the duly appointed day, Donald made his way to the dockside and found that his family and friends were there before him. His mother and George Poole had made the journey from Rota and were there with James, now a young man, and his sisters Mary and Hilda, two very attractive young ladies in their own right. So too were Hamish with Annette and their daughter, still a tiny baby.

Everyone was feeling nostalgic and the farewells were long and sincere. "Donald please take care of yourself. America is so far away, be sure to write to us." His mother was hugging him as she spoke, she gave him a final kiss, "God bless you son, please take care of yourself, you have made me very proud with what you have But if it does not work out you know we would want you to come straight back," she said, as they made their way along the dock side. The ship before him was larger than the one the families had travelled on, yet in some respects it was very similar. It had masts and sails as before but it also had funnels, indicating engines. This crossing was going to be faster. As he made his way up the gangway he thought about the last time he had boarded a ship in Oban when he had been confined below decks. Now he was a jewellery designer, and with the sale of his home in Cadiz he felt financially secure. He was directed to a very nice, but small cabin one deck below. This time he was even given a steward! There was a porthole which was well above the water level and he was able to see that there was still activity on the dock side. The cabin was simply furnished; there was a bunk and a table set with a large bowl of fruit, a jug full of fresh water, against the wall there was a built in wardrobe ready for his many clothes. Donald returned to the deck and stood at the guardrail, waving to his family and friends as the ship left the quay and made its way out of the harbour. Once at sea he returned to his cabin to unpack until there was a call to dinner; this was really going to be a very different voyage to his earlier one.

He entered the dining room and was seated at a small table set for one, there were other tables all set for couples. As he sat down a gentleman came forward to introduce himself, "Good day. My name is John Seagrave and this is my wife Helen." Donald stood to shake hands with them, "My name is Donald Grant." "Donald I am sorry I expected to hear a Spanish accent. Your name is Scottish is it not?" "Yes, I am originally from Scotland. My mother would not allow me to lose my native tongue?" he said jokingly. The trip took a full month, during which time he looked back on his life in Cadiz. Had he made the right decision? What would his life have been like if Maria had not died? What would his child have looked like, would it have been a boy or a girl? These thoughts haunted him and deprived him of many nights sleep, but he felt that he owed it to Maria to make a success of his new life. He became popular with the other passengers. A ship of this size is a very small place and it only carried a handful of passengers, who could turn out to be useful contacts for him when he tried to set up business in this new country. He was particularly friendly with John and Helen Seagrave. John was a man in his fifties, his wife was younger and showed a great interest in the fact that he was a jewellery designer, just the person to assist in the establishment of the dream that he carried with him to America. The Seagraves money had been made during the gold rush of 1849. John was the son of old Bill Seagrave. A joiner who had made his fortune providing accommodation for the miners; they had done the digging he had built their shelter. He continued to made money right up to the end. When the gold fields were abandoned Bill moved east and started a building company in New York. With the growth of that city he had become a very rich man. Bill was now dead and John was in charge of the company, but unlike his father he was enjoying a life of luxury that was the envy of many. Another couple on board, Joseph Robertson and his wife Jeanette were friends of the Seagraves; Joe was a furrier with large premises in central New York. He too was about fifty and had been a furrier all his life; he had arrived with a great many others from Scotland as a child. A victim of The Highland Clearances, as a young boy he had been encouraged to learn a trade and he had chosen the fur trade. In time he was able to start his own business in a rented back room, and through prudent judgement, had succeeded in building a thriving business in the best part of the city.

CHAPTER 13

Donald stood on the deck with the others as they entered the Hudson River and was able to admire the skyline as they approached the dock. His mind was racing. As a young boy he had said that he wanted to go to America, and here he was. His family and his friends were not with him' neither was his wife whom he had had to leave forever in Cadiz. Once ashore, Donald sought out a hotel room in the centre of the city. He entered his room and after looking round and thanking the porter he lay down on the bed and closed his eyes. His thoughts took him to Cadiz, to Maria and his family. He had no idea how long he lay there but eventually he rose and made his way to the dining room. A few days later he decided to walk round the city. He found that the streets of New York were bustling with hundreds of people all in a hurry. He had been told that Maiden Lane was the jewellery quarter of the city so he made up his mind to seek it out. He had also arranged to meet Helen Seagrave for lunch so he decided to stroll round and cut through a narrow street called Wall Street. He caught a horse cab to a new restaurant near Park Avenue in the city which was run by Chinese; the meal was different from any he had ever eaten and found that the unusual flavours were very tasty. Helen was charming as usual and after some small talk said, “Have you decided what you are going to do?” “I have had a look around and it seems to me that I should try to get premises around Fifth Avenue. What do you think?” “That would be a good idea. They are building a new block not far from there; it's very near Union Square. It could be just the place for you, have you made any contacts yet?" "No, I only know you, John and the Robertson's. Nothing has come up yet, but I'm hopeful." There was silence for a moment, and then Helen said, "How about an article in the New York Times? I know one of the editors; your story of the Countess sending you and your family away from Scotland, making your name as a jewellery designer in Cadiz; it will be a great human interest story and will give you publicity." Donald was elated at the suggestion, "would you do that? Do you think that would work?" "Well it's worth a try. You get your premises and I'll have a word with my friend," said Helen. Donald spent the next few days looking round real-estate offices and finally secured premises on the first floor of 109 Fifth Avenue.

A week later an article appeared in the New York Times telling the story of the young boy who was deported from Scotland to Australia; was shipwrecked off the coast of Spain and became a famous jewellery designer in Cadiz! Now here he was in New York at 109 Fifth Avenue, ready to serve the needs of the citizens of New York City. After that things did start to happen. John Seagrave arranged for some of his own workers to build Donald's workshop, and Helen was the first customer, although she did not actually place an order. She turned up at Donald's new premises where she found him at his drawing board, the craftsmen were fitting out his counter and benches to his instructions and to fill in time he had begun to set out new designs to make as stock. Helen peered over his shoulder and was intrigued to see the way he began his design. The shape of a bracelet soon became visible. It was made up of links set with amethyst and diamonds. And they were in the shape of a fancy scrolled letter "M". One link up and the next upside down, each joined to the next one with a gold hand set all in amethyst. Helen was intrigued, "Let me be your first customer. Make that bracelet for me please, I must have it. But could you put in sapphires instead of amethyst?" Donald hesitated. He was glad to get the sale but he had made his design in honour of Maria, whose engagement ring was amethyst and diamond. Although he was now quite fond of Helen, he had not really wanted to make an amethyst item for her, making it with sapphires was alright. Helen was his first client but others followed and Donald was on his way to becoming an established jeweller in New York City. Joseph Robertson was another who helped at the start. His wife was also fond of jewellery so he ordered a necklace; Jeanette came into the workshop where she and Donald spent a great deal of time together. The final design was a fringe collarette set with seed pearl and peridot, the pale green of the peridot blended with the yellow of the gold and the white of the pearls. Helen and John Seagrave had become good friends with Donald and often invited him to visit their home; they introduced him to their friends and to the theatres of Broadway. One evening, John took him to a dinner in Delmonico's, where he was introduced to a number of important people, including a Mr Andrew

Carnegie, who was big in steel in the state of Illinois. Soon Donald's order book began to fill. He had made up several pieces as samples and he had also been busy with his drawings, so that when a prospective customer called, he preferred to call them clients, he was ready to offer them at least an idea of his talents.

CHAPTER 14

In order to concentrate on building his budding business he checked out of the hotel and rented an apartment on the East Side. This meant that he could come and go to his workshop at all times, very often he would be working on a design until midnight. Donald got to know the other tenants in the building and found that there were four jewellers on various floors. One of them approached him in the hallway and thanked him for drawing attention to the address. As a result of the newspaper article all the jewellers in the building had benefited. During the conversation with Donald the man told him that he could get a good supply of gem quality stones from dealers in Arizona. Donald thanked him for the information; he had not wanted to upset his neighbours as he knew that one day he may have to call on them. A year later and Donald was becoming quite well known in New York. He was beginning to recoup some of the savings he had had to spend to become established as a name in jewellery design, and he felt that things were beginning to look up. It had been an eventful year; business had been slow in the beginning and very difficult to bring in cash despite an excellent start with the newspaper story and meeting some of New York dignitaries. One evening in conversation with Helen he mentioned that he used to go horse riding in Cadiz. Helen said, "But you can ride here in Central Park I go there from time to time you can hire a horse from the stables and ride most mornings. When you have a free morning let me know and I'll introduce you." Not long after, he and Helen went to one of the stables and set out for their first trot round the park. Soon he was a regular horseman in Central Park usually alone, but often joined by Helen. John and Helen had introduced him to theatre and opera. He had been to the theatre in Spain, but now he had the opportunity to see some of the best actors and singers in the Metropolitan Opera House, one of the world's greatest theatres. They had proved to be wonderful friends, when after three years in business Donald talked over the possibility of buying a house, they offered to help him in his choice. They found a house nearby. It was fairly large and stood in gardens which had been well cared for and were well established. He decided to buy it and settle down as a home owner in suburban New York. They also invited him to dinner parties where he met again some of the people who had been at the Delmonico's restaurant dinner the year before. While in the coach on the journey home Donald felt that he should return the compliment and invite some of these people to his home for and return the compliment. "Helen, I would like to give a dinner for these kind friends but I would need a hostess. Do you know anyone whom I could approach?" Helen thought for a bit then suggested, "What about Jenny Robertson, you know Joe and Jeanette's daughter?" I don't think I've met her. How old is she? Do you think she would suit?" replied Donald. "Well we will see if she is willing first. She is about twenty four. Why don't you have a word with Joe see what transpires?" He met Jenny at Helen's home. The two of them chatted for a time and then Donald asked her if she would be willing to act as his hostess for a dinner party he was about to give. "I'd love to! "Replied Jenny, "I'm not too sure what I would have to do but I'll have a talk to Helen and take it from there." Donald was relieved; he liked Jenny as soon as he saw her. He was looking on the proposed dinner party as a business arrangement as well as a social event.

The dinner was a great success, altogether there were ten guests making a dozen at table. The drinks before the meal were served by a young waitress supplied by the catering company, and the main course was served by four waiters dressed in black tie and tails. The thought crossed Donald's mind that the gulf between the small house in Strathgowan, the hunger on that awful trip in the wagon from Dalmhore to Fort William and this dinner was enormous. The guests left about 10 o'clock and Jenny and Donald sat down to chat. "I'd like to thank you, Jenny, for being such a wonderful hostess; I would have been lost without your help." "Donald I only made sure that the guests were seated, you kept them amused with your stories of Spain." "That was just telling the truth. It is not pleasant being shipwrecked but I suppose it is of interest." He paused, "if it hasn't happened to you."

Jenny laughed at this comment and said, “Well it does not seem to have harmed you too much, but it must have been quite frightening at the time. What was Scotland like?” Donald started to tell Jenny about his life in Scotland and why he had finished up in Cadiz. Before they knew it was past midnight. “I’ll get you a horse cab,” said Donald. He picked up the telephone the latest addition to his household, and called for a cab which arrived shortly after. He ushered Jenny out as the horse drawn cab arrived and apologised for keeping her so late. As Donald had hoped the dinner for special friends was a great help, he knew that he could not have done it without Jenny.

His business continued to grow. He was slowly being recognised by the public as a talented jewellery designer. He was sticking to his designs based on Scottish flowers, plants and the shapes of puddles which gave the drawing an abstract feel. He now added local flowers found only in America. The Art Nouveau styles were now being seen in all forms, mainly from Denmark, but American versions were also appearing and Donald tried to be at the forefront of this latest fashion. He recreated the flowers and ferns that he could remember, in designs of gold and silver, some with precious gemstones and some all metal. He was always very aware of his competitors, one of whom seemed to be doing better than others; he decided to keep a sharp eye on what Tiffany’s were up to. He also started to design silverware such as plates, cups and a complete range of cutlery all with the Art Nouveau theme. They were produced for him by Sam Cottle a local silversmith, slow to start but gradually they started to move enough to justify them remaining in the collection. One evening after dinner with Helen and John, the conversation came round to sailing, “We have a boat up in New England, and are going there next weekend. Why don’t you join us?” That would be great, thank you I’d love to.” “Would you like to bring a friend to make it a foursome? What about Jenny?” “I’ll see if she would like to come”.

Donald asked Jenny and she agreed to go so they were able spend a pleasant weekend with their friends off the coast of New England. The only drawback was that it gave Donald flashbacks of his earlier sailing trips and his shipwreck; he was torn between the need to overcome his fears and the need to relax with these very kind friends. After what had turned out to be an enjoyable weekend, he found that his thoughts turned to his family still in Spain. Especially his mother who was now becoming quite elderly; he made up his mind that he should write to her as soon as he got back home. His mother’s reply eventually came, as a child in her native Strathgowan she had never learned to read or write but her husband George Poole read Donald’s letter to her and had written her reply. She said that she would love to come but that she would have to see that his brother and sisters, who were still at home, were alright and then she would be delighted to travel over as soon as possible. Donald was disappointed that she could not come sooner but settled down to wait for her visit and continued to build his business.

He was walking with Jenny down Fifth Avenue when he noticed that there was a shop about to close down. "What do you think Jenny?" he said. "Do you think I could take over that shop and become a retailer?" "I don't see why not Donald. It would open you up to more New Yorkers, you have something to offer but most people do not even know that you exist". That was enough for Donald and he started to make enquiries, contacting his lawyer and talking to the bank. In April the Donald Grant store opened in Fifth Avenue. Donald had transferred his studio and workshop to premises above the new shop, John Seagrave had again arranged for the shop fitting and used his many contacts to supply all the necessary benches and specially made counters. He was standing beside his senior assistant as she opened the door for the first time. Behind him there was an array of champagne bottles and glasses ready to allow his customers to celebrate with him. As before one of the first to come was Helen. He was very grateful to the Seagraves, not only had they helped him in setting up in the first place but they had introduced him to Joe Roberson and then Jenny who was becoming a very important person in his life. He had prepared a brooch to the same basic design as the bracelet he had made for her when he first started in business and he presented it to her when she arrived at the shop. "Please accept this as a thank you for all you have done for me since I arrived in America". Helen was delighted with her gift and kissed Donald by way of return. The customers, old and new, came and went. Jenny had arrived during the forenoon and spent the rest of the day with Donald. When it was finally time to close and the staff check how much they had taken. It was obvious that they had had a great day. Donald, Jenny and the Seagraves went to Delmonico's restaurant for an evening meal and finished the day at Donald's house, all concerned feeling very tired and very elated. He wrote to his mother telling her about the opening day and about Jenny and how she had been such a help. He also included tickets for her and George's journey so that they would not refuse to come for financial reasons. He wasn't sure how she would take the news of his friendship with Jenny. He knew that she had been very fond of Maria; perhaps she would think it too soon. He was surprised to get her reply wishing him well in his relationship with Jenny and that she was very proud of all that he had achieved. She said that she hoped to travel to New York in the near future.

The following January, Jean and George Poole arrived in New York. As they entered the harbour area they were in awe of the giant Statue of Liberty, which stood majestically in the middle of the waterway. Donald and Jenny were on the quay side to welcome them, and after the hugs all round they made their way by horse cab to Donald's house. Donald and his mother had much to catch up on while Jenny took it upon herself to welcome George, she loved the story of a Devon farmer becoming a seaman on a prison ship and ending up marrying one of the prisoners in Spain. After a couple of days and having recovered from their journey Donald took them to see the shop and his workshops. They were introduced to John and Helen Seagrave, and especially Joe Robertson and his wife Jeanette. Joe being the son of a Scot from The Highland Clearances they had a lot in common. Donald and Jenny saw to it that they were treated to trips to the opera and on another occasion to the theatre. They were taken to all the local sights, but after a month of discovery and family friendship it was time for Jean and George to return to their home in Spain. Donald, Jenny and the Seagraves were at the dockside as they left and amid tears and hugs the ship slowly slipped away from the dock.

Not far from Donald's shop in Fifth Avenue was the headquarters of the oil magnate John D. Rockefeller. Donald was able to benefit from many of the staff becoming clients. Rockefeller himself did not indulge in such things but those of his staff who did call at the store were good spenders and were always welcomed by Donald. His fortunes continued to flourish and as in Spain now that he felt that he was financially secure he was soon able to buy a larger house on the East Side. One of the first things he did was to have another dinner party. Again he asked Jenny to be his hostess; the guests included Joe and Jeanette Robertson, John and Helen Seagrave were also invited. As the guests arrived Donald took Jenny aside and said, "Would you like to call in to the shop tomorrow and pick a ring?" Jenny gave Donald a puzzled look, "Would this happen to be a proposal Donald?" she asked, "Of course it is, would you like to be Mrs Grant?" "Mr Grant I would be delighted." With that she gave Donald a great big hug and a kiss! When they returned to the lounge where the guests were seated they announced that they were engaged. Joe and Jeanette Robertson jumped out of their seats and ran to congratulate the young couple.

CHAPTER 15

In Spain when Hamish heard that Jean Poole was going to visit Donald in the USA it made him consider his situation. He had often

thought about returning to Scotland because like Donald he still felt like a fugitive. He too had had a successful career; as a good mason he had been involved in many quality building projects and was in demand not only as a mason but for general building advice. He and Annetta now had two little girls and were comfortably off; he employed a lawyer to find out the status of the Grants and the McLeod's. He was informed that the Countess had died while they were in Spain. His agent in Scotland made enquires about the Bailie in Dalmhore and was told that he too was dead but that they could reopen the files. Hamish and his brothers and sisters waited for the results of this investigation for over two months, before they were advised that the records of the trial had been lost. This was great news for the families. Most of them had set down roots in Spain especially the younger family members who had married and settled down in their adopted country. George Poole wrote to Donald telling him of the result of Hamish's enquiries. When he received the letter Donald felt a great weight lifting from his shoulders; he was free to return to his native Scotland. She also told him that Hamish was going to return to Scotland on a visit and that she would let Donald know the result of this trip.

Donald was thrilled by the news. His wedding was coming soon and much as he would have liked, he knew that he could not join Hamish back in Scotland at this time, but he wished him a good trip. Hamish and Annetta arrived in Glasgow, and spent the night in the hotel at Central Station before taking the train to Cairnmhor. They then caught a coach to Strathgowan where they stayed in a coaching inn at the top of the main street. Hamish was amazed at the progress of the town, the main streets which were now complete. When they had been sent away his father had been a joiner on the site in the main square, it was now fully occupied and busy. The next day they called on Hamish's aunt, his uncle Willie the mason, who had been his idol had died, but his widow Aunty Maggie, still occupied the same house. When she opened the door she did not recognise the strange couple standing there, and was silent for a moment. "Don't you recognise me Aunty Maggie? It's Hamish, your nephew." "Who are you? I don't know you, Hamish died years ago," she said, determined to stop this intruder. Hamish laughed, "We didn't die, we survived and we were rescued and we have been living in Spain since then, this is my wife Annetta." Gingerly, she opened the door to admit them and having overcome her shock she sat entranced as Hamish told her of the adventures of the families since she had last seen them. "The old Countess died a few years ago," said Aunty Maggie. "So you'll have no trouble there. How about your friend, what's his name?" "Donald?" he replied, "He became a jewellery designer and now works in New York." "You mean in America!" cried Aunty Maggie. "My, you young people have done well." They talked all afternoon and as night started to fall they left Aunt Maggie's house and returned to their hotel for the night.

The next day they strolled along the banks of the river and stopped on the bridge, on the way Hamish pointed out the place where they had set their snare, crossing over the river they walked along the road towards the village of Garrioch passing as they did the estate of the late Countess. Hamish felt a shudder run through him as they passed along, the memory of the night he had spent in the cellar was very clear in his memory. As if to drive the message home to him an elderly man came out of the entrance. Dewar the gillie, who had been involved from the start, was walking very stiffly, he was obviously suffering from some rheumatic problem. "Hello, Mr Dewar," said Hamish, "remember me?" "You look familiar? But no, I'm not sure." "Hamish McLeod," he paused. "You sent us to Australia when we were caught with a pheasant, when that old bitch of a Countess used her power to bribe the beak in Dalmhore." Dewar stood open mouthed for a second. "I thought you were dead! We were told you had drowned when the ship sank." "Oh, the ship sank alright, but we were rescued. We all live in Spain now thanks to you and your pals. If you weren't an old man I'd kill you for what you did!" At that point Annetta held Hamish back as he moved towards Dewar, "No Hamish that's no good he isn't worth it." She said in broken English interspersed with words in Spanish, as she was speaking, she was dragging Hamish away from this man who had started the events all those years ago. Further along the road Hamish calmed down a bit. "I know if I hadn't been to Spain I couldn't have met you so you were right to stop me but I could kill that man." The meeting had been so upsetting for Hamish that they returned to Strathgowan instead of going on to the Garrioch.

The next day, as they were having their breakfast, they were informed that someone wished to see him. When he went to the foyer there was Dewar and another man he recognised as McDonald. "What do you want?" he demanded. Dewar and McDonald stood nervously in front of this well dressed young man whom they had been prepared to sacrifice. "We've come to put the record straight" said Dewar. "You better come through" retorted Hamish; the two men followed him to the bar at the rear of the inn which at that time of the morning was empty. "Wait here I'll be back in a minute." McDonald and Dewar fidgeted nervously as they waited for Hamish to return. They were even more concerned when an elegant lady returned with Hamish and was introduced as Annetta his wife. When they were all seated, Hamish turned to the two men and said, "Well?" Mc Donald was the first to speak, "The Countess was a real terror after her husband died; she became very greedy. She thought that too many pheasants were going missing and if any more were lost then we would be out of a job. That is why we had to take you up to the house; we would have lost our jobs. We thought that she would punish you two boys and that would be that. But when your families arrived we had to continue to keep up the punishment. When we found out that you were to be deported to Australia we were very upset, and when we heard that the ship had been wrecked in a storm and all the prisoners had drowned." He paused and took a deep breath. "You must realise that we were devastated, we have been ostracised in Strathgowan for years." When he had finished McDonald looked drained. Hamish was taken aback by the confession; he had thought as everyone had that the gillies were mostly to blame for what had happened. Now it appeared that they were as much victims as the families. Hamish looked at Annetta and said to her in Spanish, "What do I do?" "You can only forgive them Hamish and get rid of your anger. These men were only doing their job." "I know," replied Hamish "I have had a good life in Spain. I met you. I could not have had such a life here in Scotland."

He turned to the two men and said "I wanted to kill you for years. You put my family and the Grant family through hell and when that ship was wrecked we nearly all died. But you are not worth anger; I can only feel sorry for you, I pity you. Now please leave, I never want to see you again." The two men dejectedly left the inn. Hamish was aware of the sense of relief at the situation; he felt like celebrating and said as much to Annetta, she however was not of the same mind. "I think you have had enough stress for to-day" but in spite of the events that happened, Hamish was still keen to finish his trip to the area. That afternoon they again set out for the village of Garrioch. They walked along the road with open farmland on either side and soon could see the top of Castle Roy, a landmark on the approach to the village. Further along they passed a small golf course and then a large house up on a hill, further still there was on the left a brand new hotel and they could see in the distance the humpbacked bridge over the river. The following day they hired a coach to take them to Dalmhore where they enquired about the legal situation. They were told that as both the Countess and the bailie had died there was no one to oppose their return. After ten days of discovery for Annetta and nostalgia for Hamish they returned to Glasgow and sailed again for Cadiz. During the voyage Hamish and Annetta sat in the ship's lounge and talked about their time in Scotland. Annetta had a pretty good idea of what Hamish was thinking and said, "Hamish if you wish to return to Scotland I would have no objection. I found the place charming and I know that we could settle there, the grass and the trees are so green and the people so friendly that I would not object if you wished to go home." On their return to Spain Hamish wrote to Donald telling him of the events. Donald too was shocked by the message Hamish gave him about the Countess, and that he and Annetta were going to return to Strathgowan. Archie and Agnes were now elderly and with the rest of the family they had decided to stay in Spain; most of the children had married and had good jobs and many friendships.

None of the Grant family was keen to return either, so Hamish, Annetta and their two children were the only ones to leave Cadiz and start a new life in Scotland. They settled down in Strathgowan; their two children went to the school that Hamish had attended many years before. The local builders soon learned of his skills as a mason and within a few years he was able to set up on his own and the firm of Hamish McLeod was in demand for the still expanding Strathgowan. In a very short time he was employing some of the men that he and

Donald had known at school, even Mr Dewar from the estate was now working for him as a night watchman, all past history behind th

CHAPTER 16

When Donald and Jenny were married; Donald had paid the expenses for his mother and stepfather George, his brother and sisters to travel to the event. His friends John and Helen Seagrave were there and of course the bride's parents, Joe and Jeanette, looking absolutely delighted and extremely proud of their daughter. Being Roman Catholic they were married in St Patrick's Cathedral and the reception was held in the Park Avenue Hotel. The guests included family and friends of the bride and also many of Donald's best clients. After the wedding they spent a fortnight on honeymoon in New England, returning to Donald's, now their home, to begin married life together. When their daughter Jean was born he went through torture in the run up to her birth. Maria was in his thoughts a lot and Jenny could sense that he was troubled. She did her best to make him feel at ease telling him that she understood. The following year they moved to a large mansion in its own grounds. They were able to employ a few servants, and life was beginning to be very luxurious for the lad from Strathgowan. Little Jean was the apple of her father's eye and she could do no wrong. As an only child she began to behave in a spoiled manner, but Jenny soon put a stop to this, she did however agree to a small pony and soon she was able to accompany her parents as they rode through Central Park. Donald, Jenny and Jean were a close family and He was very protective of them; he had lost a wife and an unborn child and he was very aware from his own experience that things can change very quickly. Despite these concerns they were a very happy family, over the years their daughter attended the best schools and colleges and was always cheerful and a credit to her parents.

Jean Grant walked into the room. Now an elegant young lady she was of medium height with lush brown hair which came just to her shoulders, and a smile that her father thought was like a morning sunrise. She was dressed in a pale blue gown with a beautiful diamond necklace sparkling beneath her smiling face. Donald relaxed in a large leather armchair as he carefully trimmed a full Havana cigar and lit it with a spill from the glowing fire. "Hello my dear, are you looking forward to the opera tonight?" "Yes father, I have heard that it is very good," she replied. "I am certain it will be my dear it's "Prince Igor by Borodin." I'm told the story is as good as the music," he commented. "I hope so father," said Jean. She looked at her father; now in his late fifties he was still good looking although going a bit bald with a neat monk's fringe and great whiskers, he had put on a bit of weight but still looked every bit the successful businessman he was. There was a faint knock on the door. A maid appeared to announce the arrival of the coach which would take them into central New York for their evening. "Thank you Carla would you ask Mrs Grant to join us please, tell her that Johann is here with the coach." "Very good Sir," replied the young maid. Turning to his daughter he said, "Very well my dear shall we go?" Without looking back he walked to the door in time to see his wife descending the wide staircase in the hallway. "Ah Jenny, you're ready. You look beautiful my dear, shall we go?" he said as she reached the bottom of the stairs and came forward to join her husband. Jenny Robertson-Grant was now in her early fifties and the resemblance between herself and her young daughter was striking. The same smile, the same hair, though the brown was now replaced by a faint grey. Her figure was now a little more rounded, but despite the passing of years her natural elegance was still evident. She and Donald had been married for over twenty years. She enjoyed the large house, the servants who now did the mundane household duties she once did; she enjoyed the large grounds surrounding the house, having a coachman to drive them to the city, and being the lady of the house. Johan was waiting at the door with the coach to take the family into New York. They were to be guests of Lew Seth a well-known character in public service who had also been a Mayor of Brooklyn and a regular customer in Donald's jewellery store. Jean gave her mother a hug, "Mother I agree with father, you look beautiful." She took her mother's hand and walked with her to the door, Donald following behind beaming roundly. He liked to see his family content and he also liked to parade them in front of his friends and rivals at the opera; tonight would be a great event. He had every reason to be proud of himself; he had a very happy family, a successful business and good friends here in New York. The opera was a great success and as they emerged from the theatre Johan was waiting with the carriage.

CHAPTER 17

Donald, Jenny and Jean travelled to Scotland, gone were the slave type facilities of his first sea voyage, or even the small ship of his journey to America, this time they were in first class cabins on a large steamship. Travelling in style, they became friendly with some of the other passengers. One family of Mother, Father and son were returning from a visit to America, the Somerville's were from Edinburgh. David Somerville was twenty and a student at St Andrews University. Jean Grant found this young man very attractive and he in turn paid her a great deal of attention. During their voyage across the Atlantic the two became close, giving both sets of parents cause for concern. Jean and David soon found nooks and crannies on board in which to be alone, and by the time the ship arrived in Glasgow the two were very close and had agreed to write to each other. The following day the family travelled by train to Cairnmhor, they hired one of the few cars in the area to take them to Strathgowan. As they stepped out of the car they were met by Hamish and Annetta, the two men stood for a moment then they hugged each other as a welcome, but also an acknowledgement that after all these years they were back where they started. The emotion hung in the air; both wives were conscience of it and both felt a tear as they watched their husbands greet each other, and their lost youth. Hamish had arranged for them to stay in a large hotel on the outskirts of the town where they settled in and relaxed after their journey. The following day Annetta showed Jenny and Jean round the Strathgowan shops Jenny had been intrigued by them as she had only known the upmarket stores of central New York. The two men walked round the town and talked about the strange events which had brought them to this point in their lives. Hamish took Donald to meet Dewar and McDonald who again told their story, Donald could now understand the stresses which the men had been under, and like Hamish he did not blame them. That evening as the families sat down to dinner the waiter came forward to say that there was a visitor for Miss Jean Grant. Jean glanced at her parents with a puzzled look on her face, "Who can that be I don't know anyone here." She rose and walked to the foyer where her shout of joy could be heard by those waiting in the dining room.

She returned holding the hand of a beaming David Somerville, "Look who I have found" she cried, Donald and Hamish had risen to greet the young man. "Uncle Hamish this is David Somerville, we met on the boat over, and he has come to pay us a visit," "David it is lovely to see you, but how about your course at St Andrews, shouldn't you be there." Said Donald "I will have to return at the weekend but for now I thought I would try to visit Jean, and see this place that you talked so much about on the ship." "There you are father; it's your fault for painting such a graphic picture, although I now know why." David joined them for dinner and then booked into the hotel. The following day Jenny and

Annetta took a train to Inverness where the shopping was better. Jean and David said they would have a walk around the village.

Donald and Hamish decided they would have a walk to Garrioch, on reaching the outskirts of the village they strolled up the hill near the school. After a short distance they came upon a clearing in the middle of a large Caledonian pine forest. "This would be a great place to have a hideaway home" joked Hamish, Donald did not answer as he looked round the area, in his saddest moments over the years he had envisaged a place such as this, he still felt that he had been banished from his homeland, and despite the successes he had had in America, Scotland was his home. "Hamish, do you know if this land is for sale," he said thinking aloud "I have no idea Donald" replied Hamish Still in the same vein Donald said. "Would it be possible to build a house here"? Hamish looked at him. "Are you serious, have you any idea how much that would cost?" Donald did not answer. They started to walk the length of the open space, where Hamish commented "You could have an estate here there is plenty of room" "That's what I want" was the reply, Hamish stared at his friend and again said "have you any idea what that would cost?" "No but could you find out, I have been very lucky, I am a rich man, I want you to find out what you can, I am getting on and this would be just the place for Jenny and I to retire to." "Donald I will do my best to find out what I can, if only because it will be great to have you back where you belong." The two men returned to the town swapping ideas as they walked, later over dinner Donald broke the news of his plans to Jenny; she stared at him for a long moment and said, "Oh dear I thought something like this might happen, I understand Donald, I know you would like to come back here but is this not very sudden, where is this place?" Donald smiled and said "Tomorrow I'll show you, it is very secluded and very beautiful" That night Jean sprung a surprise on her parents "Mother, Father, I have decided not to return home with you. I would like to go with David to St Andrews; He thinks that I could get a job there." Donald and Jenny were horrified! "You cannot live on your own in a strange town just to be with someone you barely know!" cried Jenny, "I am only doing what Father did. I'm capable of looking after myself, and you have met his mother and father you know they are a nice family." After a heated discussion, things were left, with Donald and Jenny, hoping that Jean might change her mind. The following day they set off to Garrioch. Jenny and Donald were still upset with Jean's suggestion, but tried to put the thoughts to the back of their minds for the time being. When Jenny saw the place she realised why Donald had wished to build a house there, "I think this would be a lovely spot Donald if you think that you would like to go ahead then I fully agree, what do you think Jean?" Jean was walking ahead hand in hand with David and replied "It's awful quiet Father, a bit out of the way don't you think." She was being polite; her mind was not on what she was saying but on the young man at her side. "Don't worry Jean" said Hamish "this is a piece of ground at the moment, try to visualise it, over there you will see the drive running down towards that little stream we crossed, and at the foot of the drive the lodge house and gates, over there will be the big house and gardens and in that corner will be the servants quarters" he indicated over to his left. Donald looked at Hamish "you have been doing your homework haven't you," "Well, we have to start somewhere" replied Hamish smiling. "He sat all last night doing sketches I knew he was up to something" said Annetta. All six of them strolled round the ground and Hamish pointed out the various parts of the ground, and the sketch he had done for each particular area, they then strolled back to the town, Jean and Jenny taking in the area that could become their future home. After dinner Hamish and Donald sat in the lounge of the hotel and discussed what they would want for the interior of the mansion they planned to build. Donald sailed back to the USA alone, after a fortnight of nostalgia for him and discovery for his family. Jenny was very upset that Jean wanted to be with her new boyfriend and had said that Jean could stay in Edinburgh provided that she go with her and set up some kind of home there. This seemed like a good compromise solution as Jean would only see David at weekends and her mother and his parents would be able to keep an eye on the situation. This left Donald feeling very left out, however back in New York the routine of running an ever growing jewellery empire was a good distraction and helped alleviate his loneliness.

A few weeks after his return Donald received a letter from Hamish with a lawyers letter enclosed, it gave him the price of the ground he was interested in purchasing, Donald replied that he had instructed his bank to give the necessary assurances to complete the transaction. He was also informed that the land he was purchasing was from the estate of the late Countess of Badenoch, the irony of the situation did not pass Donald by. Jenny also wrote to him often, telling him that she had rented a small house in Edinburgh, and she was enjoying her visit to another part of Scotland, Jean had managed to get a job in a local lawyer's office, and the on-off romance between David and Jean was carried out at weekends. Eventually Hamish sent the details of the ground with a draft of the suggested plans they had discussed, drawn up by a top architect who Hamish had recommended. Donald kept Jenny and Jean informed about the progress of the work at Garrioch, they was still a bit sceptical of the enterprise, but the more the events were developing the greater his interest in the possible appearance of the main house. He tried to envisage the end result from the sketches and his now fading memory of the actual site. As time passed Donald decided that he better visit again to deal with some of the on-going problems, he trusted Hamish but the design of the house was a personal matter and he felt that he should be there. He travelled on his own this time, but had arranged to meet Jenny and Jean there, he arrived at Strathgowan, he stayed with Hamish and his family for one night, Annetta and the girls made him welcome and he was spoiled by their attention. The girls were delighted when he presented them with beautiful pendants of amethyst and diamond, each the reverse design of the other, there was also a matching bracelet for Annetta; this was quite a gift as Donald now only made amethyst jewellery for close family and special friends. Jenny and Jean arrived from Edinburgh; the family had decided to go to Garrioch where they booked in to the new hotel. The next day they returned to the estate site and were amazed by the progress that had been made. There was now a long drive up the hill which formed a circle in front of the house, or where the house would be. At that time only the foundations could be seen.

The family group with Hamish and the architect walked round these foundations and they saw that to the rear there were already indications of a garden layout. Having completed the tour of the main site they went over to the side where they were told there would be three semidetached houses for servant's quarters and also a large area for a garage. Satisfied by the progress Donald Jenny and Jean returned to New York to consider all that they had seen, Jenny was delighted and said she was looking forward to spending time there. Jean had been silent on the return voyage and after a couple of days she broke down and said that she and David had had a row and that she did not wish to talk about him anymore.

CHAPTER 18

Now it was just a matter of waiting, all Donald could do was sit at his drawing board and try to create new designs for his workshops to carry out, but he could not concentrate, his heart was back in Scotland, he could not help wondering how things were progressing. One day he said to Jenny that it would be great to get back to a Strathgowan to see the new house, Jenny joked that he was not to worry about it as Hamish had everything in hand, although she had noticed that Donald had not been himself in recent times. Jean and Jenny sat in the lounge of their home talking, Jenny said, "your father is not very happy Jean, I think it would be nice if we went back to Scotland I'm sure that is what your he needs," Jean was supportive "Yes I think so mother, sounds like a good idea why don't we go, you could book up now and tell him later as a surprise." Jenny booked passage for the family and also decided to take Johan with them, telling him that she thought that they might need his help when they got to Scotland. Donald was sitting at his desk struggling with a design which was not working out, he was looking very tired when Jenny came up behind him and said "Donald do you remember talking about going to Strathgowan, well here are the tickets we sail in two weeks" After he had got over the shock he said "Darling that sounds wonderful what a lovely surprise," When the due date arrived they walked up the gangway, but once on deck Donald gratefully sat down on a bench, "Are you alright Donald" asked jenny "Just a little tired give me a minute and we'll have a look at the cabin", after a moment Donald rose and accompanied by Johan made his way to the cabin. They had a very pleasant voyage, in Glasgow they were able to hire a car and Johan drove them all the way to Garrioch where they stayed in the new hotel. Hamish and Annetta met them there and they spent the evening chatting in the lounge, they arranged to pick up Jenny and Donald the next day to take them to the house. In the morning they drove Donald and jenny the short distance up to the new house, Johan and Jean followed in the hired car. As they drove Hamish explained to Donald that the house was ready, and needed only two things, furniture and a name. "I have the name Hamish. Altnagar" "What does that mean Donald" asked Jenny "It's Gaelic for the junction of the burn or stream in English?" They approached the wrought iron gates between the stone pillars and saw that they were at the foot of a long drive, to their right there was the lodge keeper's house which Hamish had spoken about. They rode up the drive and saw that on both sides there had been rhododendrons newly planted, at the top of the drive they came to a circle of grass in front of the house. There were lawns on either side and beyond them walls with balustrade running down either side finishing each in a small square building. “That one over there is your ice house and that’s a little gazebo for you to rest when you have walked too long in the garden”. Donald studied the outside of the building, he was pleased with what he saw; Hamish had made a good job of his new home. They approached the front door; up few steps and then Donald was able to walk into his new house, Jean uttered a ta-da trumpet sound to set off the proceedings as Donald entered his dream home. Standing in the entrance hall of the house he liked what he saw, to his left stood a very ornate marble fireplace and in front up two steps there was the double door of the lounge. “Let’s have a look around” they entered the main lounge, noted the conservatory at the rear and the gardens freshly laid out and even a fountain playing, opening a door on the left they discovered another room which Hamish said was the dining room, a second door in that room led to large well-appointed kitchens. Further along the main corridor there was the room which was designated as the library and another already furnished with a full size billiard table. Having completed the ground floor they started up the stair “Donald do take care darling you are trying to do too much” pleaded Jenny as he seemed to try to run upstairs “Don’t worry I’m fine I just want to see what we have upstairs” he said as he continued to climb, he got to the small landing half way up and rested before carrying on up. They continued to look round the entire house, and then they all crossed over to the servant’s quarters where it was noted that the gardener had already moved in. Donald knocked on the door, it was opened by a middle aged man in working clothes, “I am Donald Grant I believe that you are James Archer and that you are to be our gardener.” Said Donald “I am that sir would you like to come in,” acknowledged James “I would be delighted” replied Donald and walked into the kitchen of this small house followed by Jenny Jean and Hamish. “Mr McLeod told me that you would be coming to see your new house sir, I hope you like it, would you like a cup of tea.” “Thank you Mr McLeod did a good job James, thank you but we will not stop, thank you for your hospitality.”

Back at the hotel they sat down to have an enjoyable meal together to celebrate, and after dinner the five of them moved to the lounge to discuss the house, they decided that they should go to Edinburgh to get the furniture and linens. Hamish had all the measurements and Jenny was already planning the various pieces of furniture they would use in each of the main rooms. Two days later joined by Johan they boarded the train at Cairnmhor which took them to Edinburgh; this trip was turning out to be a bit of an adventure. Jenny was aware that the stress and excitement was affecting both Donald and Jean, Donald because the house was nearly complete and Jean because Jenny knew that she still had fond thoughts of David.

Hamish not thinking of Jean's situation said to Jenny, "He'll be alright, the journey was tiring for us all, and Johan is looking after him, I don't think you should worry too much, we'll have a quiet day tomorrow and he can rest up." The next day Donald was feeling a lot better and it was he who suggested that they take a look at the shops where they would be buying their furniture. They walked along Princes Street and were impressed by the spectacle of the castle perched on the massive rock which dominated the centre of the city. Jenny and Annetta were soon engrossed in the purpose of furnishing Altnagar house, none of them had got used to the name yet, only Donald used that name. Jean said she wanted to meet some of the friends she had known when she had lived there, and agreed to meet with them back at the hotel. Donald and Hamish crossed over Princes Street followed by Johan and entered the gardens, "Let's look down there" said Donald. They descended a flight of steps to a walkway half way down where they saw a beautiful golden fountain newly erected there. After a pleasant stroll in the shadow of the castle they came to a further set of steps leading the junction of Princes Street and a road to the castle. They climbed up to road level and found themselves back in the middle of Princes Street, having enjoyed their walk they returned to the hotel and met up with the ladies as arranged. The family with Johan in attendance returned to New York where Donald set about realising his assets, and made arrangements to invest his money. Six months later they settled into Altnagar house. They worked hard to get the house to their liking, and once settled they decided to throw a party for all the workers and friends who had helped to make the house a home. Hamish and Donald stood together praising each other for a job well done, Jean was watching them from the other side of the room and suddenly out of the corner of her eye she saw the front door open and the smiling face of David appeared. She let out a cry and swiftly crossed to him throwing herself into his arms. Jenny came over to Donald and they both watched as David led their daughter out of the room, only to return a few minutes later smiling broadly. Jean and David made their way over to her parents and as they did so Jean suddenly lifted her left hand to show a beautiful single diamond ring. Jenny and Donald were overjoyed to see their daughter so happy. They were home and their daughter was with the man she was going to marry. .

The End